When she was eleven and Gabe seventeen, she had fallen in love and made up her mind to marry him.

Dana had spent countless hours fantasizing about her best friend's big brother.

And now Gabe looked even better than she remembered. Taller. More rugged.

But it wasn't his broad shoulders or tight jeans that riveted her attention. It was the dark eyes that stared into hers until she wanted to run away again.

But Dana wasn't a little girl now. And she hadn't the slightest intention of running away. She told herself her feelings for Gabe Purvis were long gone, and he'd never had any for her.

She told herself she'd come to Iron Springs strictly to fight for little Danny's future....

But was the real reason standing before her?

Dear Reader,

Happy Anniversary! We're kicking off a yearlong celebration in honor of Silhouette Books' 20th Anniversary, with unforgettable love stories by your favorite authors, including Nora Roberts, Diana Palmer, Sherryl Woods, Joan Elliott Pickart and many more!

Sherryl Woods delivers the first baby of the new year in *The Cowboy and the New Year's Baby,* which launches AND BABY MAKES THREE: THE DELACOURTS OF TEXAS. And return to Whitehorn, Montana, as Laurie Paige tells the story of an undercover agent who comes home to protect his family and finds his heart in *A Family Homecoming,* part of MONTANA MAVERICKS: RETURN TO WHITEHORN.

Next is Christine Rimmer's tale of a lady doc's determination to resist the charming new hospital administrator. Happily, he proves irresistible in *A Doctor's Vow,* part of PRESCRIPTION: MARRIAGE. And don't miss Marie Ferrarella's sensational family story set in Alaska, *Stand-In Mom.*

Also this month, Leigh Greenwood tells the tale of two past lovers who must be *Married by High Noon* in order to save a child. Finally, opposites attract in *Awakened By His Kiss,* a tender love story by newcomer Judith Lyons.

Join the celebration; treat yourself to all six Special Edition romance novels each month!

Best,

Karen Taylor Richman
Senior Editor

Please address questions and book requests to:
Silhouette Reader Service
U.S.: 3010 Walden Ave., P.O. Box 1325, Buffalo, NY 14269
Canadian: P.O. Box 609, Fort Erie, Ont. L2A 5X3

LEIGH GREENWOOD

MARRIED BY HIGH NOON

Silhouette®

SPECIAL EDITION®

Published by Silhouette Books

America's Publisher of Contemporary Romance

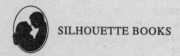 SILHOUETTE BOOKS

ISBN 0-373-24295-6

MARRIED BY HIGH NOON

Books by Leigh Greenwood

Silhouette Special Edition

Just What the Doctor Ordered #1223
Married by High Noon #1295

LEIGH GREENWOOD

has authored twenty historical romances and debuted in Silhouette Special Edition with *Just What the Doctor Ordered*. The proud parent of three children ranging in age from seventeen to twenty-four, Leigh lives in Charlotte, North Carolina. You can write to Leigh Greenwood at P.O. Box 470761, Charlotte, NC 28226. A SASE would be appreciated.

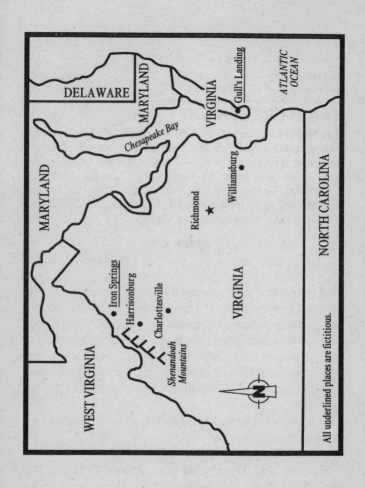

All underlined places are fictitious.

Chapter One

As she slowly drove down the single street in the tiny mountain community of Iron Springs, Dana Marsh felt like she was stepping back into the past. She hadn't been here in fourteen years, yet nothing had changed. If it hadn't been for the little boy sleeping in his car seat behind her, she would have felt that she was a teenager again, coming to spend the summer with her grandmother.

In the town that had betrayed her. She'd sworn never to come here again.

"Wake up, darling. We're here."

She was glad Danny had slept almost the entire trip from New York. He still didn't understand that his mother's sudden death a month earlier from cancer meant he'd never see her again. He asked for Mattie all the time, especially at night. Dana hadn't wanted to change his routine by uprooting him from his home so soon, but his uncle had insisted that she bring him to Virginia the minute he recovered from his fever.

Dana pulled her Jaguar to a stop in front of a two-story, white, clapboard house.

"Want juice," Danny announced.

Danny had his mother's soft Southern accent rather than the sharp edge of Dana's New York inflection. Even though Danny wouldn't be two for another month, he could already talk as well as a four-year-old. That didn't surprise Dana. He had a brilliant executive of a Fortune 500 company for his father, and an innovative artist for his mother.

"Let's wait until we get inside," Dana said.

He still wasn't potty trained. She didn't think her initial meeting with Gabe and his lawyer would be the best time to change a wet diaper. She expected Gabe would cringe in disgust. Why should he have any ability to understand a child's feelings, even his nephew's? He hadn't understood hers when she was sixteen.

She got out of the car and opened the back door.

"I'll get you out of this nasty old car seat. You'll soon be able to run around to your heart's content." There had to be some advantages to living at the ends of the earth. There were plenty of safe places to play.

She took Danny out of his car seat and carried him up the steps of the tall, stark-white house built in the shape of an L. It used to be mostly hidden by trees and vines, but the trees had been trimmed, the vines pulled down and the overgrown boxwoods pruned to a manageable size. Marshall Evans opened his door before she could ring the bell.

"You're late," Marshall said.

"Sorry, but I can't gauge the exact length of a trip from New York," she said as she stepped inside.

Dana had forgotten that Marshall's house was filled with Victorian furniture as valuable as it was ugly. She wondered if he would sell her a few pieces. She had a client who was heavily into Victorian. She told herself to forget antiques. She had come to fight for Danny's future. She was also on vacation. Her doctor had ordered her to take a complete break from business.

"Where's Gabe?" she asked as her eyes adjusted to the dimly lit interior. Marshall had pulled the heavy, floral print curtains together to shut out the sunlight.

"In the kitchen," Marshall said, turning in that direction and leaving her to follow.

Everything was backward here. In New York people entertained in the living room. In Iron Springs, only strangers sat in the parlor. Dana passed through a second parlor, a dining room and an old-fashioned butler's pantry. Enough antiques to set up an entire showroom.

Dana didn't get a chance to look at the kitchen. Gabe Purvis rose from the table when she entered the room, banishing all thoughts of antiques from her mind.

Shock sent the past thundering down on her like a rock slide. One summer, when she was eleven and Gabe seventeen, he had winked at her as he handed her a cone of butter pecan ice cream. She had fallen in love then and there and made up her mind to marry him when she got out of college. She'd spent countless hours fantasizing about him, prying details about him from his sister. Mattie had laughed at the notion of her best friend marrying her brother, but Dana thought he was the most wonderful boy in the world.

Gabe looked better than she remembered. He had grown taller and had filled out. He looked more rugged, more solid. Despite the season, he wore a checkered shirt rolled up at the sleeves, tight jeans and heavy work shoes. But it wasn't his clothes that riveted her attention. Nor was it his broad shoulders and powerful forearms, which she supposed came from lifting heavy lumber and wrestling with large pieces of furniture. It was his face that defined his character, his powerful jaw and wide forehead, shaggy brows and weather-roughened skin, thick, nearly black hair that refused to be tamed. And black eyes that stared into her until she wanted to run away.

But she wasn't a little girl now. Even though she hadn't wanted to come back, she hadn't the slightest intention of running away.

Gabe's gaze moved from her to Danny. "Is that my nephew?"

"Of course." She shouldn't have snapped at him, but her nerves were on edge.

She hadn't been unduly upset when she first learned Mattie had made Gabe Danny's joint guardian with her. She'd assumed a thirty-six-year-old bachelor wouldn't want to be burdened with a small child. She would agree to take Danny to Iron Springs to visit Mattie's family during vacations, might even let him spend a few summers there, but she had every expectation of having the child to herself.

Gabe had exploded that belief.

Not only had he insisted that she bring Danny to Iron Springs the minute the boy recovered from his fever, he said Mattie's stipulation that Danny be raised near his family meant he had to *live* in Iron Springs. Dana's lawyer had advised her to work out a compromise with Gabe, but Dana doubted she could. She had come to Iron Springs ready to do battle.

But right now she had to calm down before she upset Danny. He'd had more than enough change in his life.

"Sorry," she said. "It was a long trip to make with a small child. On top of Mattie's death...well, I'm still strung out." She couldn't think of Mattie without wanting to cry all over again.

She still found it hard to believe anyone as young, vital, and healthy as Mattie could be diagnosed with cancer one day and be dead three weeks later. For twenty-five years, they'd been closer than sisters. Mattie had come to live with Dana when she'd learned she was pregnant. They'd gone through morning sickness together, doctors' appointments, lectures on prenatal care, Lamaze classes, endless discussions about what to name the baby. Dana had been at Mattie's side in the delivery room. She'd placed Danny in Mattie's arms. They'd sat up together on nights when he had the croup or a fever, had taken turns walking him when he couldn't sleep, had shared the tasks of feeding, bathing, changing diapers.

Danny had become part of Dana's life, her soul, but now everyone expected her to hand him over to his uncle and go back to her old life as if these past three years had never happened. Losing Mattie had been like losing part of herself. That made her all the more determined to hold on to Danny.

"Let me have him." Gabe held out his arms, but Danny buried his face in Dana's neck.

"Not yet. He doesn't know you."

"He'll have to get used to him sooner or later," Marshall said. "He might as well start now."

"He'll start when I say." She could hear the anger in her voice. She tried to control her tone, the rigidity of her body, but she couldn't help it. The thought of giving Danny to anyone filled her with an anger at the whole world that was as red-hot as it was impotent.

A knock at the back door came as a welcome distraction. A woman accompanied by a young boy let herself in. "I'm Naomi Ferguson," she said, introducing herself. "This is my son, Elton. I suggested to Marshall that Danny might be happier if I took him off to play while you and Gabe discussed business. Would you like to play with Elton?" Naomi asked Danny.

He hid his face in Dana's shoulder again.

"I'll look after him," Elton said, swaggering like a little man.

Trying not to grin, Dana squatted down until Danny and Elton were eye-to-eye. "Danny's a little shy. He doesn't have anybody to play with at home."

"He don't have to be scared," Elton said. "Won't nobody say boo to him if I tell 'em not to."

"I'll keep an eye on both of them," Naomi said with a wink.

As reluctant as Dana was to let Danny out of her sight, she knew it would be better for everybody if he were at least in another room while she talked to Gabe.

"Do you want to go with Elton?" Dana asked Danny.

The child eyed Elton curiously but didn't relinquish his hold on Dana's neck.

"You can have some of my cookies," Elton offered. He reached inside one of the deep pockets of his baggy pants and withdrew a plastic bag full of chocolate chip cookies. "Mama made 'em," he said as he took one out of the bag and offered it to Danny. "Can't nobody make better cookies than Mama."

The cookie was a sad little thing, bent and twisted from its time in Elton's pocket. Apparently its sad state didn't bother Danny. He reached for the cookie.

"I got more," Elton said reaching into another pocket and drawing out a second bag of cookies. "I'll get some milk, and we can go sit on Marshall's porch and eat the rest of them."

The lure of two handfuls of cookies was too much for Danny. He loosened his grip on Dana and slid to the floor. Elton held out his hand, and Danny took it. "You don't have to worry about your kid, lady," Elton said to Dana. "He's safe with me."

Naomi laughed as Elton and Danny headed toward the back door. "No child can resist chocolate chip cookies," she said as she opened the cabinet and took out two glasses.

"I think it was Elton," Gabe said.

Naomi took milk from the refrigerator. "I'll keep them on the screened porch."

Dana couldn't stop herself from looking through the window. Danny had settled next to Elton, munching on a cookie, looking up at the older boy with wonder in his eyes.

"Your son is an angel," she said to Naomi.

"Only sometimes," Naomi said, then closed the door behind her as she joined the kids on the porch.

Dana took one last look, turned to face Gabe.

"Why don't you leave now?" Marshall asked. "You could be halfway to the interstate before he finishes his cookies."

His suggestion was so unexpected, so completely without any regard for Danny's feelings, Dana couldn't think of the words to tell him what an unfeeling idiot he was.

"We have some things to talk over," Gabe said.

"A lot of things," Dana said, recovering her speech. "Not the least of which is this absurd notion you have that you can take care of Danny as well as I can. You don't know anything about children. Why did you force me to bring him to Iron Springs?"

"Because Mattie wanted him to live here."

"She didn't say that."

"She wanted him brought up with his family. That doesn't mean New York."

"I could send him down on vacations."

"No."

"Maybe even summers."

"He lives here. I'll let him visit you during summers and vacations."

Dana's lawyer had already warned her not to expect more than this, but she couldn't accept the thought of being separated from Danny for months at a time. "He ought to live in one place with somebody he knows, somebody who knows how to care for him. That's obviously me. How are you going to take care of him? Where is he going to stay?"

"I have a house. Naomi will keep him during the day. He'd have to be in day care in New York. And for much longer hours, considering your job."

Dana's lawyer had pointed that out, too

"He doesn't know you or anybody else here."

"You don't have to worry about that," Marshall said. "Gabe can—"

"How can I not worry?" Dana said. "He's lost his mother, he's been sick, he's been taken away from the only home he's ever known, and you want me to turn him over to a perfect stranger and disappear."

"I don't see—"

"Then you're blind," Dana snapped.

"Nothing's going to happen to him except you leaving," Marshall said. "He'll probably cry, but he'll get over it."

Dana fixed Marshall with a look she hoped conveyed what an unfeeling cretin she thought he was. "I'm not relinquishing one bit of my responsibility for Danny. Mattie made me joint guardian. I wouldn't consider leaving him with Gabe for as much as an hour until I know he can take care of him. And I won't be easy to convince."

Gabe opened his mouth to speak, but Dana plunged ahead. "I did my best to convince Mattie to give Danny to me."

She paused to collect herself, to stop the tears before they filled her eyes. She'd promised herself she wouldn't lose her temper and wouldn't cry. She'd done one and was about to do the other. But losing Danny so soon after Mattie's death would be more than she could bear. After all the worry, love and laughter they shared, she didn't know how she could stand to be alone again.

She opened her handbag to look for a tissue. Gabe handed her his handkerchief. She hesitated only briefly before taking it to wipe her eyes. Touching him set off a reaction she'd never felt before. He radiated a vitality that drew her like a magnet. She tried to throttle the unwelcome current of excitement that surged through her. She told herself not to be a fool. Her feelings for him were long dead. He'd never had any for her.

She swallowed, took a deep breath, then looked directly at Gabe. "Mattie didn't give me full custody of Danny because she said a boy ought to have a man he could model himself after. Of course that's nonsense, but I couldn't convince Mattie."

She waited for one of them to argue, but neither did.

"I don't know why you can't leave him with me." Her eyes started to water again, and she buried them in

Gabe's handkerchief. "He's got his own room. Toys. People he knows."

"He can have all that here," Gabe said.

"You could visit him in New York."

"You haven't let us see him, not even after Mattie died."

"I'd have brought him to Mattie's funeral if he hadn't been sick." Though she knew Mattie would understand, Dana couldn't stop feeling guilty that having to stay in New York with Danny had caused her to miss Mattie's funeral.

The phone rang. Dana and Gabe both turned to Marshall, but he didn't move. It rang again.

"Answer it," Gabe told Marshall. "Dana and I can handle this ourselves."

The phone rang again, and Marshall left the room. Much to her surprise, Dana felt herself tense. Surely after all these years she could face Gabe without being uncomfortable.

"Before I can think of letting you have Danny for a single night," she said, "I've got to know you can take care of a little boy who's hardly more than a baby. What do you know about children? Have you ever been around any?"

"I don't know a lot, but I don't anticipate any difficulty learning."

"Well I do," Dana shot back. "You don't know what he likes, what he doesn't, what frightens him, what to do when he gets upset. You don't know what foods upset his stomach, what he tends to gobble, what he has to be coaxed to eat, when he should go to bed, when to start potty training." She threw up her hands. "Leaving him with you would be practically the same as leaving him with Elton."

"I'm a little more capable than that," Gabe said.

His smile surprised her. She'd expected a snarl.

"Mattie didn't know how to take care of a child," Gabe said, "but she learned. I think I can, too."

"She was a woman. You're not." Gabe probably thought if a poor woman could manage, a man would have no difficulty. Just thinking about it made her angry. "Who's going to take care of Danny while you're at work?" she asked.

Gabe signed. "I've already told you Naomi will take care of him during the week. My mother can help out if I have to be away on weekends."

"If Mattie had wanted him raised by strangers, she could have left him with me. If you had a wife, it would solve everything. Are you engaged?"

"No."

"Do you have anybody in mind?"

"I'm not engaged, I don't have anybody in mind, and I intend to raise Danny without a wife."

He acted as though having a wife was about as desirable as contracting mumps, but her own reaction upset her more. She could deny it if she wanted, but knowing he was still single excited her.

"I don't see why you want to know all this."

"Because you're expecting me to let you have the child I love," Dana said. "Did you think I could just drop Danny off and go back to New York as if nothing ever happened?"

"I didn't mean—"

"Well I can't. He's been part of my life since the day Mattie moved into my apartment. You might as well ask me to give up my own child."

"Are you married?" Gabe asked.

"No."

"Engaged?"

"No."

"Anybody on the horizon?"

"Why do you want to know?"

"As far as taking care of Danny is concerned, you're no different from me."

"Not true. I know him. You don't."

"I'll learn."

"In how many years?"

Gabe laughed. "I promise to figure it out before he graduates high school."

"I don't know how you can take this so lightly. We're talking about a child's life here, not some...some piece of furniture. You don't put it together, polish it up and hand it over to somebody else."

Apparently she'd finally succeeded in angering him. His brows lowered and puckered. Any hint of a smile disappeared.

"Danny is all my mother and I have left of Mattie. Making sure we do everything right for him is just about the most important thing in our lives. Now call him in from the porch. We can take his things over to the house and settle him in. You ought to be able to start back to New York tonight."

Dana couldn't believe her ears. Hadn't he heard anything she'd said? "I have no intention of turning Danny over to you this afternoon. Or tomorrow afternoon, for that matter. Mattie gave me equal custody. That means I have equal right to approve all arrangements."

"Satisfying you could take days," Gabe said.

"I'm sure it will. That's why I've taken two weeks vacation."

Gabe stared at her very much in the manner she would

have expected if she'd grown a second head right before his eyes.

Marshall returned to the room in this interval of silence.

"She's not going to leave," Gabe said to his lawyer. "She's going to stay here for two weeks, sticking her nose into everything I do, complaining and demanding."

"You've got more important things to worry about than Dana," Marshall said.

"If you think—"

Gabe interrupted Dana. "What are you talking about?"

Being cut off angered Dana, but Marshall's expression caused her to choke off her outburst.

"That was Lucius Abernathy, Danny's natural father, on the phone."

Dana had been looking over her shoulder ever since Mattie's death, afraid he would show up again demanding Danny.

"His lawyer is flying to Washington tomorrow," Marshall said. "He plans to rent a car and drive to Iron Springs."

"What does he want?" Gabe asked.

"Danny," Marshall answered.

"Mattie's will specifically says we're to be his guardians," Dana said.

"An uncle and a friend won't stand much of a chance against the natural father."

"Is there anything we can do to stop him?" Gabe asked.

"Maybe."

"What?"

"I'll do anything," Dana added.

"Gabe's best chance to keep Danny is to get married before the lawyer gets here."

"But he said he didn't have anybody in mind," Dana pointed out.

Marshall looked straight at her. "I know. So since you're willing to do anything to make sure Danny's natural father doesn't get him, I suggest you marry Gabe."

Chapter Two

Marshall couldn't have stunned Gabe more completely if he'd suggested he have a public drawing to choose his wife. Even if he were foolish enough to consider remarriage, Dana Marsh would be the last woman he'd choose.

Not that she was hard to look at.

He remembered her as a skinny kid with huge brown eyes, sun-browned arms and legs, honey-brown hair that was always getting in her face. As often as not, she had a tear in her clothes and dirt on her chin. She could assume a look of doll-like innocence or change to a pixie-full-of-mischief in the blink of an eye. Despite the hard feelings some locals still harbored against her mother, she could charm nearly anyone into a sunny mood.

But he could see nothing of that innocence in Dana now.

She had turned into a New York siren with a body to die for. Dressed and accessorized with understated but expensive taste, she represented nearly everything he had come to distrust in a woman. At thirty-six years old, mature and experienced, he should have been beyond the impressionable age. Then why did his heart beat as if he'd just run the four hundred? He should be shouting down Marshall's impossible suggestion that he marry Dana, but all that blood flooding his brain made it impossible to think.

"You're crazy," Dana said, finding her tongue before Gabe. "I wouldn't marry Gabe if he were the last man in the world."

"You both want to keep Danny," Marshall said. "Gabe has to get married to have a chance. It's the obvious solution."

"There must be another way."

"Maybe, but you've got less than twenty-four hours to find it."

"You're the lawyer," Gabe said. "You're supposed to find the solution."

"I have," Marshall replied.

"You can't seriously expect us to get married just like that," Gabe said, snapping his fingers. "We haven't seen each other in more than fourteen years."

"And we can't stand each other," Dana added.

That was going too far for Gabe. Dana might figure in his mind as the human embodiment of everything that had gone wrong in his life, but a man would have to be a misogynist to have any difficulty *standing* a woman like Dana.

"We have some differences of opinion," Gabe said.

"I'm not saying you have to love each other," Marshall said. "I'm just trying to come up with a way for you to keep this kid. If you don't want—"

"Don't be a fool," Gabe snapped. "You know I want him."

"Then you have to get married. It's almost impossible for an uncle to win custody over the natural father, especially when the natural father is a wealthy, respected businessman with a wife and family ready and willing to welcome Danny into their midst."

"Even if the natural father got furious when Maggie told him she was pregnant," Dana said, angrily, "ordered her to get rid of the kid, and walked out when she wouldn't?"

"Even then. Today's courts lean heavily on the side of the natural parents."

"He only wants Danny because he's a boy," Dana said.

"You can't prove that. As far as the court is concerned, it would be the perfect situation for Danny, certainly better than living with a bachelor uncle who has to put him in day care. We'd have even less chance if he lived with you."

"I could hire a live-in housekeeper." Gabe said.

"You couldn't afford it," Marshall said.

"I'll pay for it," Dana offered.

"It wouldn't matter where the money came from," Marshall said. "It's the family unit the judge is going to consider."

Dana looked at Gabe. The look felt almost accusatory. "Can't you find somebody to marry?"

"Not on twenty-four hour's notice."

"Maybe Marshall could get the judge to wait longer. If you could just—"

"There's nobody I want to marry," Gabe snapped,

"not now, not in twenty-four hours or twenty-four days."

"I guess that brings it back to you two," Marshall said.

"You heard what he said," Dana said. "That *nobody* includes me."

"You don't have to want to get married. You just have to do it. You can file for divorce as soon as the judge hears the case."

Gabe looked at Dana. She glared back at him. He would never consider marrying her under normal circumstances. But if he couldn't keep Danny any other way, he could put up with it, particularly if they got a divorce as soon as he got custody. If the natural father got custody, he would never see his nephew again.

"Can a person get married that quickly on a Saturday?" Gabe asked.

"Not normally," Marshall said, "but there are ways."

Dana jumped up and headed toward the door to the back porch.

"You can stop looking at me like that," she said. "I'm not doing it. I'll take Danny back to New York first."

"There's no way the courts will give him to you," Marshall said.

"You can visit him anytime you want," Gabe said.

"Do you think his father will make you the same offer?" Marshall asked.

Gabe could tell from her look she knew he wouldn't. He could also tell she felt caught between two desperate choices, neither of which she felt she could accept. If she was to give Marshall's idea even five minutes' serious consideration, he had to find a way to take some pressure off her.

"Why don't we get Danny and head over to my house so you can see his room?"

She looked relieved to have something else to do, thankful to him for having suggested it. He could understand. After years of burying himself in his work and not allowing himself to feel anything—not bitterness over his wife's betrayal and subsequent divorce, not anger at the rift that tore his family apart—he felt buried under an emotional landslide. His father's and Mattie's deaths coming so close together had demolished his emotional barriers. Danny's arrival made him feel even more vulnerable. Now, years of bottled-up emotions bubbled to the surface. He, too, needed time to sort things out.

"Why?" Marshall asked.

"Dana said she wouldn't leave Danny with me until she was perfectly satisfied I could take care of him. Checking out the suitability of where he'll live ought to be high on the list."

"What about the lawyer hired by Danny's father?" Dana asked.

"Let's work on the assumption we're keeping Danny."

Dana nodded, opened the door and went out to the back porch.

"Do you think she'll do it?" Marshall asked.

"I don't know. It was a terrific shock."

Marshall laughed. "I thought all women swooned at the thought of marrying a hunk like you."

"She nearly did."

Both men laughed, but Marshall sobered quickly. "What about you?"

"It'll only be for a few weeks or a couple of months."

"I wondered if after Ellen…"

"This isn't the same."

"You got that right. Dana isn't a lying, deceitful witch. If she's going to shaft you, she'll tell you right to your face."

"Why don't you fix your sidewalks?" Dana asked.

They were walking back toward the heart of the community, the street and lawns shaded by huge oaks.

"We like them cracked and uneven," Gabe replied.

"A person could break a leg."

"Half the town learned to walk stepping over them."

"Strangers didn't."

"We don't have many strangers. And those we get stay at the ski lodge or go straight to the camp."

"How about the people who come to the hotel?" she asked, referring to the huge, pre-Civil War building with wide verandahs on all three levels that towered over the surrounding houses.

"People come to the hotel to get away from their ordinary lives," he told Dana. "They like the cracks in the sidewalks, the sixteen-foot ceilings, the rocking chairs on the verandas. Some of them come back every year just to sit and rock for a whole week."

"I couldn't stand that," she said.

"I know."

She whipped around. "What to you mean by that?"

He didn't know how she walked in those heels without stumbling, though he had to admit they set her legs off to good advantage. Of course her legs would have looked good even if she'd been barefoot.

"Are you going to answer me, or are you going to

stare at me as if I'm a piece of wood whose grain you're judging?''

He grinned. "You're much finer to look at than any piece of wood I've ever worked with. As for your grain—''

"I didn't intend for you to take me so literally.''

She became uneasy under his scrutiny, looked away hastily, moved ahead quickly. It pleased him to know a country boy could rattle a woman used to the fast lane.

"We should be talking about Danny.''

Danny scampered along ahead of them, peeping through fences, walking in the bottom of the dry ditch, peering into drain pipes. He didn't have any trouble with the sidewalk. Whenever a piece of concrete tilted a little too high for him to step on the crack, he jumped it. But he stopped frequently to make sure Dana followed close behind.

"Okay, we'll talk about Danny.''

But talking about Danny wasn't safe, either. It brought up Marshall's preposterous idea. Gabe still couldn't believe he'd suggested it. People didn't do things like that anymore. Still, Gabe couldn't dismiss the thought of marrying Dana.

He didn't know what kind of suit she was wearing, or what kind of material it was made of, but he did know he'd never seen anything cling to and outline a body more effectively. Each time he dropped back to allow her to precede him where shrubs overhung the sidewalk, he marveled at her long legs, slim hips and small waist. He didn't care if it came naturally or if she spent twenty hours a week in a gym. He practically had to clench his fists to keep from reaching out to touch her.

"How did Danny get along with Elton?'' Gabe forced

himself to walk alongside Dana, his gaze on Danny just ahead.

"Fine as long as the cookies lasted," she replied. "Naomi said he seemed a little lost after that."

"How come?"

"He doesn't know how to play. He hasn't had a chance to be around other children."

Gabe couldn't deceive himself into thinking the boy would soon forget Dana. Despite Marshall's advice, he had no intention of attempting to tear Danny from Dana's arms. If he and his mother wanted to be equally important to this child, they had to give and earn similar feelings of love and security. Gabe doubted two weeks would be enough.

Seeing how much Danny loved and depended on Dana—how deeply she was attached to him—forced Gabe to amend at least part of his opinion of Dana. She was obviously warm and nurturing in her relationship with Danny. Being separated would hurt Danny as much as Dana. Maybe more.

"Did you have a good time with Elton?" Gabe asked Danny.

Danny nodded, ducked his head, ran back to Dana and hugged her around the legs. She picked him up, and he wrapped his arms tightly around her neck. She didn't seem the least bit conscious of the damage done to her expensive clothes.

Gabe wasn't sure he could afford to think about Dana's good qualities. The moment he did, visions of having her naked in his bed turned his thoughts to charcoal. He could forget her seductive charm as long as she stayed in New York, but he had trouble remembering the dangers of being attracted to a woman like her when she walked just ahead of him.

If he had half a brain, he wouldn't think about that at all. A beautiful, smart, aggressive career woman, expecting to get anything she wanted, she came dangerously close to being like his ex-wife. Whether he wanted to admit it or not, he was more attracted to Dana than to any woman he'd met in more than ten years. Being told he had to marry her in order to gain permanent custody of Danny merely gave his libido license to go into overdrive.

"Danny will get along with the other kids just fine," Dana said as she set Danny down again. He started forward, walking on the cracks. "All he needs is a little time. Mattie and I both thought he was too young to go to play school."

Gabe didn't think Danny was upset so much as clinging to someone familiar in strange situations. But until he got to know his nephew, he couldn't be sure what the child needed or wanted. For the time being, he'd have to depend on Dana. And he would listen to her advice. He wanted the very best for his nephew.

"Why don't we stop at Hannah's for ice cream?" Gabe asked.

"It'll spoil his dinner."

"I don't remember it ruining yours," Gabe said with a sudden smile. "And you had it often enough. I dished it up, remember?"

"Want ice cream," Danny said.

"Now see what you've done."

Gabe chucked Danny under the chin. "What kind do you like?"

"'Nilla."

"I won't have you trying to buy his affections," Dana warned.

Gabe felt a spurt of anger, but he supposed in a way that's what he was doing.

"I've got to start somewhere, and I don't have any chocolate chip cookies. I have to go inside the store to get the ice cream," Gabe said to Danny. "You want to go with me?"

Gabe held out his finger. Danny sidled closer to Dana.

Gabe wanted to bend down and scoop the child up into his arms, but he remained perfectly still, waiting, his hand outstretched.

Finally yielding to the lure of ice cream, Danny hesitatingly reached out and took hold of Gabe's finger.

Gabe was stunned by the feelings that surged to the surface. He'd played with dozens of children, but never had a child's taking his finger caused him to tear up. Danny looked so much like Mattie he could hardly stand it. Gabe's throat tightened, and he swallowed.

Gabe held out his other hand. "Want me to carry you?"

Danny hesitated, looked at Dana.

"Go on," Dana urged. "I'll be right here."

After a moment Danny held out his arms and Gabe scooped him up. The little boy felt tiny and fragile in his arms. Gabe shifted him to his right side, and Danny put his arms around Gabe's neck. Gabe knew it was only to hold on, but his feelings intensified. He was strongly loyal, but he'd never suspected himself of being sentimental.

It was the purely emotional reaction of a man to a child who shared his blood. He guessed it was something left over from primitive man's instinct to care for and protect members of his family. It had to be instinct. It had come from nowhere to completely engulf him, but it felt good.

"Want cone," Danny said.

One look into the child's trusting eyes and Gabe was no longer interested only in proving himself to Dana. He wanted to prove to Danny that he loved him, that Danny could trust him, could always count on him.

Dana stayed behind as Gabe and Danny started up the steps. Remembering how Hannah jammed the rows together until there was hardly room to walk between them wasn't the reason she didn't go inside. She wanted to be alone. Danny's going to Gabe, even though he'd done so only because she encouraged him, had upset her. Another reminder that she was losing him.

She loved Danny, and she wanted him to be happy, but it tore at her heart to see him go to anyone instead of her.

Marry Gabe and you can be with Danny forever.

She didn't know where that little voice in her head came from, but it might as well go away. Nothing could convince her to consider Marshall's ridiculous suggestion.

Thank goodness Gabe hadn't pushed it. She couldn't believe Marshall had had the nerve to suggest it. She wanted nothing to do with Gabe or Iron Springs. She told herself the instantaneous attraction when she walked into Marshall's kitchen represented nothing more than a healthy woman's response to a handsome and virile man.

The tiny voice somewhere deep inside her head kept whispering that this might be her only chance to get what she'd always wanted. She couldn't convince that tiny voice she didn't want it anymore.

Even though she had passed her thirtieth birthday and could practically hear her biological clock ticking, she didn't feel desperate to find a husband. The fact that all the men she dated seemed to be like her father—obsessed with business, short on time for her, unwilling to commit and uninterested in a family—didn't discourage her. Older women had more trouble getting pregnant and delivering a healthy baby, but New York doctors could do wonders these days.

Still, she couldn't put the idea of marrying Gabe out of her mind. She was a partner in a business that dealt in very pricey antiques. Despite her family's contacts, it had been difficult to build up a clientele. She had figured out that one way to attract a woman's attention to a valuable antique was to have a handsome man sit or lean on it. In five years, she had worked with virtually every top male model in New York. Put up against them, there wasn't a woman in her right mind who wouldn't choose Gabe.

It was impossible not to be attracted to him. His smile, when he bothered to smile, was devastatingly sexy. It was a little crooked, one side of his mouth a little higher than the other. He tilted his head ever so slightly, and his eyes sparkled. His lips—those full, wonderful, sexy lips—parted to reveal a set of teeth worthy of any toothpaste commercial. The women in this place must be blind not to have hauled him off to some dark cave long before now. *She* had known he was something special from the first moment she saw him twenty-five years ago.

She had been a nervous five-year-old visiting her grandmother for the first time. He'd been behind the counter in Hannah's store. He was eleven. He looked so big and handsome and confident when he winked and gave her an extra big scoop. After that she'd gone for an ice cream cone every afternoon—for the next eleven summers.

Dana pushed the memories from her mind. She couldn't afford to turn nostalgic. At this rate she'd soon *want* to marry him. That thought caused a tiny pool of heat to coil in her belly.

"I keam," Danny cried, as he burst out of Hannah's store, his double scoop of vanilla leaning perilously to one side of the cone. Some of the ice cream dripped on her blouse when he threw himself into her arms, but she didn't care. Having him run straight to her meant more than a dozen blouses.

"Don't blame me for the double scoop," Gabe said. "That was Hannah's idea."

She looked up to see Gabe holding two cones. "Your favorite, butter pecan," he said as he held one out to her.

"I didn't want one."

"Hannah remembered how you could never come to the store without begging your grandmother for a cone. She figured you might still like it."

Smiling, Dana accepted the cone. "It's still my favorite."

Hannah came out of the store. "That's a fine looking boy," she said, "the spitting image of Mattie. You staying long?"

"Long enough to help settle Danny in," Dana said. "We're going to see his room now."

"Gabe's got a beautiful place," Hannah said before going back inside.

Dana headed off at a rapid pace. Danny ran alongside.

"Don't be in such a rush," Gabe said, sauntering along behind her. "It's too hot to hurry."

"From what Mattie said, you never come out of your shop long enough to know the season, much less the weather."

"Mattie exaggerates. Exaggerated."

He tried not to show it, but she saw the lines of pain in his face. She wanted to let him know she understood, but she didn't know how.

They walked down the middle of the street, eating their ice cream. She couldn't imagine such a scene in New York. She kept veering toward the sidewalk, but Gabe continued down the middle of the road. After a while she gave up. She hadn't see a car since she arrived. "Where is everybody?" she asked.

"Probably napping. We're between sessions at the camp and the hotel. The new campers and a group of folk dancers will come in tomorrow afternoon. Until then we've got the place to ourselves. Isn't it wonderful?"

It would be if there were any reason to live here, but she didn't say that to Gabe. He loved this town. He crossed the street and started up a short sidewalk.

"I thought old Mr. Wadsworth lived here," she said.

"He did. But his children didn't want the house after he died, so I bought it."

Dana couldn't imagine why Gabe should want such a large house. She walked inside and came face-to-face with an enormous grandfather clock. The hand work was incredibly intricate.

"I'm surprised one of the Wadsworth children didn't want this," she said.

"They did, but I wouldn't sell it."

"Why would their father sell it to you instead of leaving it to one of them?"

"It wasn't his to leave. It's mine. I made it."

Dana had always known Gabe handcrafted furniture, but she'd never expected anything like this.

"Did you make any of these tables?" she asked.

There were four in the hall, all with ball-and-claw feet. The carving alone must have taken days.

"I made all the furniture in this house," Gabe said, waiting for her to follow him.

Dana's gaze turned to a dining room she glimpsed through pocket doors. It contained a huge mahogany table surrounded by six chairs. A sideboard stood against the far wall next to a china cabinet. She crossed the hall into the living room. Tables, corner cabinets and a table-model grandfather clock offered mute proof of Gabe's considerable skill. She wondered if he had any idea how much all of this would be worth on the New York market. She doubted he knew or cared.

"Come on," he called. "You can poke around in corners later."

A porcelain-topped kitchen table with pull-out leaves restored her feeling of how Iron Springs ought to be—old-fashioned, out of date, comfortable. She immediately found the paper towels. She tore off several pieces, dampened them under the faucet and washed Danny's face and hands.

"Me, too," Gabe said, holding out his hands just like Danny.

Marshall's preposterous suggestion came crashing back with the force of an exploding bomb, and paralysis held Dana still for a moment. She jerked herself back into reality. She didn't intend for Gabe to see how badly his joke had shaken her. "Sure. What's one more grubby little boy?"

But touching him, holding his hands while she washed away the nonexistent ice cream, caused a recurrence of the agitation that had attacked her earlier. "Can you cook?" she asked, hoping to distract herself from the uncomfortably disturbing feeling.

"Sure. I've been cooking for myself since my divorce."

She'd been expecting him to say he ate at his mother's house. "Show me Danny's bedroom."

She followed Gabe up a staircase that curved along three sides of the front hall. The windows on the upper landing offered wide views of the front and back yards as well as provided a cool breeze.

"You ought to air condition the place," Dana said, pushing aside the thought that living in this house could be very pleasant.

"I have, but the trees keep it cool most of the time."

"How many bedrooms do you have?"

"Five."

"Why so many?"

"That's how many came with the house."

She didn't appreciate his sense of humor. "Danny will feel lost."

"I bought it when I still expected to have a large family." He said it as though his shattered dreams didn't matter anymore. He opened the door to one of the rooms on the front. "This will be Danny's."

Dana stepped into a room at least twice the size of Danny's bedroom in her apartment. Gabe had furnished it with a bed, a chair and table, two chests of drawers, an armoire and two boxes spilling over with toys. Danny wiggled past her.

"Where did all of these toys come from?" Dana asked.

"All over. Everybody wanted to help when they heard Danny was coming home."

Danny bypassed the boxes of toys for a hobbyhorse in the corner. Dana didn't think anybody had such a toy anymore. She instinctively knew Gabe had made it.

"Horsey," Danny said, pointing at the hobbyhorse.

"Do you want to ride?" Gabe asked.

"Yes."

"Say please," Dana added without thinking.

"Pease," Danny said.

Gabe moved to lift Danny onto the horse, but Danny ran to Dana. "Want Danie," he said.

Danny still loved her, wanted her, trusted her. Right now that meant more than anything in the world.

If you marry Gabe, you can have Danny with you forever.

The voice lied. They'd both demand a divorce the moment Gabe got permanent custody of Danny.

"He's still nervous about all the changes and new people," Dana said as she lifted Danny onto the hobbyhorse.

"That's understandable."

Dana could tell Danny's reaction hurt Gabe. But if his family was so important to him, he shouldn't have let his father close Mattie out of their lives.

If you marry Gabe, neither of you has to be hurt.

Before the voice had the chance to drive her mad, they heard footsteps downstairs.

"Gabe, are you here?" a voice called out.

"Up here, Ma. We're in Danny's room."

In less than a minute a tall, matronly woman with iron-gray hair, glasses and a busy print dress that nearly gave Dana hives entered the room. Mrs. Purvis looked extremely nervous about finding herself face-to-face with Dana.

"I was sorry to hear about your husband," Dana said.

"Thank you," Mrs. Purvis responded. An awkward silence followed. "Thank you for bringing Danny," she finally said. She waited, looking even more uncomfortable. "And for taking care of Mattie. We...Gabe and I..."

"She was my best friend," Dana said. "I would have done anything for her." She still couldn't understand how any mother could allow herself to be cut off from her child.

She sensed Mrs. Purvis had suffered terribly, suffered still. The older woman smiled sadly, as though accepting the implied guilt, but when she turned her gaze to Danny her entire countenance was transformed.

"Why didn't you tell me he was here?" she demanded of Gabe, planting a kiss on Danny's head and rocking the hobbyhorse so vigorously Dana was afraid Danny might fall off.

"Because I knew you'd take him away the minute you saw him," Gabe said, smiling fondly at his mother, "just as you're doing now."

Mother and son bent over the child, making over him like doting parents. Dana stifled an urge to elbow them aside.

"We need to think about dinner," she said. She'd planned to eat at a restaurant or up at the hotel.

"You're eating at my house," Mrs. Purvis said.

"She's been planning what to cook for days," Gabe said. "She's changed her mind three times already. We can't stay too late," he warned. "Danny needs to get to bed early."

"I don't think he ought to sleep in this room tonight," Mrs. Purvis said.

"Why not?"

"It's too new, and he's too far away from you."

"He could sleep in my room."

They were talking as if she wasn't there, as if she didn't matter.

"You don't have to worry about Danny being alone," Dana said. "He's staying with me."

"I don't want him staying at the hotel," Gabe protested.

"He won't be," Dana replied. "We'll be staying at my grandmother's farmhouse."

Chapter Three

"You didn't have to come with me," Dana said to Gabe. "I still remember the way."

"Nobody goes to that house anymore. No telling what you'll find there."

Dana appreciated his company. The farm lay ten miles out of town.

"Nothing more intimidating than a fox or two," she said.

"More likely a raccoon or an opossum."

Dana didn't like the sound of that. She should have thought before she left New York to call the real estate agent and have her check over the house. But trying to figure out how to keep from losing Danny had filled her mind to the exclusion of everything else.

"Do you want me to drive?" Gabe asked.

"Why?" The road curved abruptly as it wound its way through the hills.

"You're not used to driving in the mountains."

Dana laughed. "I spend at least a month each summer in the Adirondacks. Sometimes, after driving a particularly mountainous stretch of highway, I feel as though I never want to go back to flat roads. The sense of freedom is intoxicating."

But that's not how she felt about *these* mountains. They gave her an empty feeling. She couldn't understand why Mattie had insisted her son be raised in the very place Mattie had been determined to leave behind. There was nothing for anybody to do here except work, talk and take naps. Dana didn't understand why such a handsome, intelligent man as Gabe hadn't left years ago. Surely he had some ambition.

"It shows," Gabe said.

"What?" His voice scattered her thoughts.

"Your experience driving in the mountains. You drove that section like you've been doing it all your life."

It was a rather insignificant compliment, but Dana found herself quivering with pleasure. She told herself not to be silly, that she was no longer a little girl desperate for the approval of a handsome older boy.

As they neared the entrance to the lane leading to her grandmother's house, Dana caught sight of the little red barn mailbox. She felt a lump in her throat. She used to beg her grandmother to let her get the mail just so she could open the sliding door.

"I need to get someone to paint that mailbox," Dana said, noticing the colors had faded badly.

"Why? There's nobody here to get mail."

That wasn't important. What mattered was that the mailbox look the way it always had. She couldn't explain that to Gabe because she couldn't explain it to herself. She had thought she hated Iron Springs, never wanted to see the farmhouse again. Yet one look brought a wealth of memories surging to the surface, good memories she had forgotten.

The mailbox didn't bother her as much as the neglected appearance of the driveway. Grass and great clumps of weeds grew through the loose gravel. A bank of tall weeds and bushy shrubs leaned into the driveway, seeming to block the entrance to the farm, telling people to stay out. Dana didn't remember the trees being so tall. Their outflung branches would soon meet overhead.

"It looks deserted," she said.

"It is deserted. No one's lived on the place since your grandmother died."

Her grandmother had died of a heart attack during Dana's senior year in high school. Dana's mother had wanted to bring her to New York for burial, but Grandmother Ebberling's will had been very specific. She was to be buried in the Iron Springs Cemetery alongside her husband.

"I thought someone rented the land."

"They used to, but it's hardly worth the effort to farm these days. They wanted to fence the fields and turn them into pastures, but your lawyer wouldn't authorize the money. Nobody's used the place for five years."

Dana had left all arrangements to the family lawyer. "It was supposed to be kept in order," she said.

"Not according to your rental agent, Sue. She keeps asking for permission to make changes so it can be rented out again, but your attorney refuses to authorize any expenditures beyond making sure the roof doesn't leak."

Dana knew she was as much to blame as the lawyer. Her parents wanted her to sell it, but she kept putting off making a decision. Her grandmother's will had stated that Dana was to have the farm so she would always have a place to call home. Dana hadn't understood why the daughter of a millionaire father needed a farmhouse in order to have a home.

"A couple of people tried to buy it, but the lawyer said you wouldn't sell," Gabe said.

Couldn't was more accurate. She'd started to several times, but something always stopped her. She prepared herself to see the house surrounded by weeds and vines growing up to the second floor. Surprisingly, the lawn had been recently mowed.

"Who cut the grass?"

"Sue has her son do it once a month. She met her husband at one of the parties your grandmother used to give when your mother was a girl. She got her first kiss under the oak near the back meadow. With all those memories, she said she couldn't stand to see the place go to ruin."

Dana made a mental note to repay Sue. She pulled the Jaguar to a stop in front of the house. Danny couldn't wait to get out of his car seat, but Dana didn't want him out of her sight.

"This house is in no condition for you to stay here," Gabe said.

"Probably not," Dana agreed, "but I won't know until I look inside."

Suddenly she knew she wanted to be alone when she entered the house.

"Swing!" Danny cried.

Memories of the swings flooded back poignant and strong. She and Mattie used to swing side by side for hours, talking about anything that came into their minds.

"I'm not sure it's safe," Dana said.

"I'll check," Gabe said.

"How?"

"I'll sit in it. If it holds my weight, it'll hold Danny."

Danny didn't draw back when Gabe held out his hand, but he made no move to take it and leave Dana. As much as his clinging to her gratified Dana, she knew her own feelings weren't the ones that mattered now. She might hate it, but Danny's future depended on his being able to trust both his guardians, to be happy living with either. If she loved this child as much as she believed, she'd do everything in her power to help him learn to love Gabe.

But having good intentions was easier than living up to them. A part of her hoped Danny would always love her better than Gabe. That made her wonder about her own character. She'd always considered herself a generous person. Being selfish wasn't good for Danny.

Dana knelt down in front of Danny and forced herself to say, "Why don't you go play on the swing with Gabe? I have to go inside and see how many spiderwebs have been built since I was here a long time ago."

Danny continued to cling to Dana, but not so tightly.

"If we go down to the fields, we might see a deer," Gabe said.

"He doesn't know what a deer is," Dana said. She could tell from Gabe's shocked expression he probably thought she was guilty of criminal neglect in the boy's education. "Gabe will swing you," Dana coaxed. The idea seemed to appeal to him. When Gabe reached out and took Danny's hand, he didn't pull away.

"Won't you come with me?" Gabe coxed.

"Go on," Dana urged. "I'll be out in a jiffy, then you can push me in the swing."

Danny's smile was immediate and brilliant. "Danie not swing."

"I did, too," Dana said. "Your mama and I used to swing all the time. We'd have competitions to see who could go higher."

"Who won?" Gabe asked.

"I did," Dana replied, suddenly self-conscious.

"I thought so," Gabe said. He smiled, but Dana had the feeling she'd just confirmed some point in his poor opinion of her.

"Danny swing," Danny suddenly announced. "Swing high."

Not too high, Dana mouthed to Gabe.

"We'll swing you up into the tree," Gabe said. "Then you can look in all the birds' nests and see if they have any eggs. Robins lay bright blue eggs. Have you ever seen a robin's egg?"

"No," Danny said as he looked over his shoulder to assure himself Dana was still there.

"Have you ever climbed a tree?" Gabe asked.

"People not climb tree," Danny announced. "Monkey climb tree."

"Little boys climb trees, too," Gabe said. "I've got a perfect tree at my house for climbing. Tomorrow I'll show you how to get up in it."

"Way high?" Danny asked.

"Way high," Gabe replied.

That bribe melted Danny's resistance. She guessed that was part of what Mattie meant when she said a little boy had to have a man in the house. Dana wasn't ready to admit a woman couldn't do at least as well as a man, but it was clear men had an unfair advantage in some areas. After all, what grown woman wanted to climb a tree?

Dana turned toward the house. When she reached the steps she looked back. She wondered how high Gabe would let Danny climb. She wondered if he'd be able to see across the fields. She didn't remember that she'd ever climbed a tree when she was a girl. She wondered why not.

The porch ran the full length of the front of the house. At one end the same old swing moved ever so slightly in the stiff breeze that came up from the valley below, but the half dozen chairs where her grandmother had rocked while she visited with her friends had disappeared. So had the flower boxes of petunias, the pots of ferns and baskets of begonias trailing long ropes of vivid red, pink and orange blossoms. Her grandmother had been particularly fond of her flowers. The porch didn't look right without them.

But Dana was in for an even bigger surprise when she unlocked the door and stepped inside. Though the neglect was obvious, everything looked so much the way she'd last seen it fourteen years ago it gave her a terrific jolt. She could almost expect her grandmother to call from the kitchen to ask if she and Mattie wanted molasses cookies or hot soda biscuits with fresh butter and blackberry jam. The weight of memories was so sudden and so enormous—memories of warmth, happiness, closeness—Dana wondered how she could even think about selling the house that had been a home as much as a haven.

Dana didn't doubt her parents loved her, but they were always coming home from somewhere, getting ready to leave again. Her father traveled constantly to or from one of several foreign countries to oversee his business interests. Her beautiful, smart and talented mother jetted from one high-profile social or charity event to another.

They owned three apartments and two vacation homes, all professionally redecorated every two or three years. Nothing ever became old or familiar. Her grandmother's house never changed and her grandmother was always there.

Always.

Dana had forgotten how much she looked forward to summers here, how much she had depended on her grandmother for feelings of belonging and permanence, for the show of affection her parents were too busy to give, for the chance to be herself, to not have to measure up to anyone's wishes or expectations. In the years since her grandmother's death, she'd gotten so busy trying to build a career successful enough to attract her parents' attention she'd forgotten what this place had meant to her, what her grandmother had provided for her without her even being aware of it.

It was the only place she'd ever been completely happy. She guessed that was the reason she'd never been able to sell the place.

Now Mattie and her grandmother were gone, and the house was all she had left to remind her of some of the best moments of her life. She couldn't sell it. Not ever. She would fix it up. It would be a place to stay when she visited Danny.

If you marry Gabe, you won't need a place to stay.

If Dana could have gotten her hands on that miserable little voice, she'd have strangled the wretch. She had been under too much stress lately to think dispassionately. Coming here had merely added more layers of emotion, many strange and unexpected, all in conflict. She couldn't possibly marry Gabe, even for a short time. That would throw her entire world into chaos.

But she couldn't let Lucius get Danny. She'd promised Mattie she'd do anything she could to prevent it. When she made that promise, she hadn't expected the solution to be so drastic. Improbable. Impossible. Insane.

Marriage should be forever. Despite the large number of divorces and separations among her friends, Dana had always been certain it would be different for her. She would know Mr. Right when she saw him, and he'd know her just as certainly. They wouldn't be anything like her own parents. They would come home to the same house every night, eat dinner together, go out together, vacation together, raise their children together. Dana wanted at least three children. Being the only child of absentee parents had been very lonely.

She looked out the window and saw Gabe pushing Danny in the swing. Even though a tangle of weeds and vines ringed the yard, the scene touched her deeply. It seemed right. Much to her surprise, some of the tension seemed to leave her. She supposed Danny's laughter and Gabe's happiness had communicated itself to her.

But there was something else going on between those two, something she could only partially understand. Gabe was obviously working hard to win Danny's trust, talking to him, laughing with him, helping him experience something new. But there was a look on Gabe's face Dana hadn't seen before. If she hadn't known better, she would have said Gabe was acting like a proud and loving father on an outing with his son.

Danny looked different, too. Though he laughed like any little boy laughed when having a good time, he looked up in wonder at the big man who was devoting his entire attention to him. His look seemed to say he wanted that very much but feared it a little at the same time.

Dana shook her head. All this intense emotion was

causing her to imagine things. She lived in the real world, not in a fairy tale where everything always had a happy ending.

But even though she focused her mind on inspecting the house thoroughly—even the room she'd called her own for so many summers—the image of Danny and Gabe together wouldn't leave her mind. Maybe she wasn't imagining things. Maybe even stories in the real world could have fairy-tale endings.

When she came outside again, she didn't see Danny or Gabe anywhere. For a moment panic caused her heart to race. Then she told herself not to be foolish. Gabe wouldn't let Danny out of his sight, wouldn't let anything happen to him. But her heart climbed into her throat once more when she walked around the side of the house and still didn't see them. Hearing voices coming from the side yard in the vicinity of a huge white pine, she worked to regain her calm as she walked across the coarse grass.

She bent down to pass beneath the branches of the pine. But they weren't under that tree. The sounds came from the old maple just beyond. They sounded as though they were coming from somewhere above her. She looked up, and a scream nearly ripped from her.

Gabe sat perched on a limb at least ten feet off the ground. Danny was seated on a branch above him.

"Don't you think that's a little too high?" She didn't know how she managed to sound so calm. She wanted to scream that Gabe was an idiot and order him to bring Danny to the ground this very minute.

"We were looking for a break in the trees so Danny can see the mountain on the other side of Iron Springs," Gabe explained.

Under other circumstances Dana might have been intrigued by the possibility of seeing Iron Springs from her grandmother's maple tree. "Maybe you should wait until the leaves fall," she said to Gabe. "Then you won't have to climb so high."

"Climbing high is half the fun," Gabe called down.

"Wait until he's a teenager."

"Tree," Danny called to her, pointing to the surrounding branches.

"I see it, darling, but it's time to come down now."

"Stay in tree," Danny said.

"We'd better come down for now," Gabe said. "I've got a bigger tree at my house. Would you like to climb that with me?"

"Me climb big tree," Danny said.

Dana made a silent vow to cut that tree down herself before she'd let Danny climb it.

Gabe dropped to the ground. When he held his hands up, Danny jumped into them without a moment's hesitation. The second Gabe set him in the ground, he came running to Dana.

"Me climb tree," he announced as he threw himself into Dana's arms.

She grabbed him up and held him tight, relieved to have him safely on the ground. If Gabe thought she was going to leave Danny here just so he could risk his precious little neck by letting him climb every tree in Iron Springs, he had another think coming. She'd take Danny back to New York and fight Lucius herself. If she didn't win, she could seek refuge in her parents' apartment in Paris. She could always sell antiques in France. The country was full of them.

"How did things look inside?" Gabe asked.

She didn't want to talk about the house. She wanted to talk about his callous disregard for Danny's safety.

"Except for a thick layer of dust, it looks very much the way I remember it."

"It's still in no condition for you to occupy."

"I realize that. I'll just have to say in your house. You can go to a motel."

She hadn't meant to say that. It just popped out of her mouth. From his expression, she guessed it surprised him as much as it did her.

"It's important for Danny to start getting used to your house. It would be better if he could do it with me close by."

If you marry Gabe, Danny will always be close by.

She shook her head vigorously, hoping to fling the maddening little voice into the grass where she devoutly hoped it would be nibbled to death by voracious ants.

She managed to get her racing thoughts under control. "I didn't mean to commandeer your house like that. I was just thinking out loud."

"No problem," Gabe said, but he looked as though it were anything but all right. "I can spend the night with Ma."

"Maybe Danny and I should go to your mother's house."

"No. The sooner Danny gets used to his bedroom, the better."

But he won't be able to spend many nights in it if you don't marry Gabe.

Dana began to wonder what part of her mind could take such sadistic enjoyment in torturing her. Nothing like this had ever happened before. Why should it be happening now when she was at her most defenseless?

"We'd better head back to town," Gabe said.

"Why?"

"Mother's expecting us for dinner. She'll worry herself into a fit if we're a minute late. What did you decide to do about the house?''

"I'm going to keep it.''

"What for? You haven't used it in fourteen years.''

"I'm going to fix it up for myself. I can stay there when I visit Danny.''

An uncomfortable silence fell. She could practically read his thoughts, but right now she couldn't take the blame for Lucius getting Danny. She'd had too much to endure these past weeks. One more thing just might be too much.

"Why did you stay in Iron Springs?'' she asked.

Chapter Four

She hadn't meant to ask that. She resented it when anyone asked her such a personal question.

"Why should I leave?"

She could think of a hundred reasons. "Mattie said you did very well in college, that you had two promising job offers."

"I discovered I'd rather work with wood than be an engineer."

"But you could do that anywhere. Why come back here?"

"Why go anywhere else?"

"Mattie couldn't wait to get out."

She hadn't meant to say that. She didn't know if he knew how his sister felt about Iron Springs, but she figured learning wouldn't improve his attitude toward her. A glance at his profile—the rigid jaw and pursed lips— told her she'd judged correctly.

"Being with people I know and trust is important to me." Gabe stared straight ahead. "I met lots of people in college who considered me their friend, but it wasn't the same as with people around here."

"Why not?"

"Because they only knew me for a few years, a semester, even a month. The people here have known me since I was born. They knew my parents before that, their parents before that. It's like a large family. If anything happens to one of us, it happens to everybody."

Dana could believe that. Her mother had made a lot of people in Iron Springs angry before she left for college. Years later, when Dana visited her grandmother, they still remembered. *She's a Yankee, poor thing. You can't expect anything better of her.*

"I wanted to stay near my family," Gabe said. "After Mattie went away, Ma and Pa didn't have anyone but me. I liked being able to walk to my parents' house before breakfast, or have them visit me."

"Most people don't want their parents that close."

"To me it's a privilege. There's nobody more concerned for me, more willing to lend a hand if I need it. I can't always depend upon friends. I can on family."

Dana's life had been entirely different. Even in grade school, her parents had been away from home more often than not. When she went away to boarding school, college, started work, they sent cards, talked on the telephone, kept in touch by e-mail, but they maintained their separate lives. Dana couldn't think of anything more unlikely than her mother showing up at her apartment before breakfast. Her mother never got out of bed before 10:00 a.m.

"I like familiar places," Gabe continued. "I can't go anywhere without being reminded of something I really like doing, somebody important to me. If I left Iron Springs, I'd lose all that."

Dana opened her mouth to argue, then closed it again. Coming back to Iron Springs had brought to the surface many memories she'd forgotten. But stepping into her grandmother's house had been almost like becoming a different person, someone she used to be but hadn't been in a long time. She hadn't expected that, wouldn't have believed it an hour ago. She had left a great chunk of herself in Iron Springs, and she hadn't realized it until now.

"I like the slower pace," Gabe said. "Everybody's not after you to do 10 percent more this year than you did last. We don't have to justify everything to cost accountants or efficiency experts. If I need to take the afternoon off, I just close up my shop. I also like selling things I make to people I know. Every piece of furniture I make is designed with a specific person in mind. I know what they like, what they need, even where it'll go in the house. It's nice to be able to see how close I came to finding the perfect solution."

Dana could understand that. She'd often wondered where a particularly beautiful antique would be placed, if its setting would complement the piece. Even repeat customers seldom invited her into their homes.

"Maybe most of all, I like being around people I can trust, people who consider me part of their own family. People buy furniture from me even though they could get it cheaper at a discount store, because they know I'll work a little harder to give them what they want. That's a wonderfully warm feeling. It may sound trite in this day and time, but it makes my work more fun because it adds meaning to everything I do."

Dana had never looked at things like that. Everyone

she knew subscribed to the theory that you ought to do ten percent more this year, fifteen if you could manage it; that you shouldn't worry about anything but making the sale; that numbers were all that counted; that you weren't a success unless you were a success in other people's eyes; that if working fifty hours a week was good, working sixty was better; that everything in life was secondary to being successful. She had to be a huge success to force her parents to recognize her achievements.

She had done all that and more.

Before Mattie came to live with her, she'd never once questioned that she was doing exactly what she wanted. But after Danny's birth, she found her job at odds with being able to spend as much time at home as she wanted. Despite her partner's objections, she stopped working sixteen-hour days, seven-day weeks. She'd even gotten to the point where, while she was trying to make a sale that might have netted them as much as fifty thousand dollars profit, she'd be thinking of what she meant to do after she left work.

Then Mattie got sick, and the worry and fear made Dana impossible to live with. Her partner had been relieved when Dana's doctor ordered her to take some time off. Neither of them considered it anything but a temporary situation. But Gabe's remarks, coming after her visit to her grandmother's house, had reshuffled things in her head, had put them together in a way she'd never looked at them before.

In the world's eyes—admit it! In hers, too—Gabe was a failure and she was a great success. But even with a failed marriage in his past, Gabe was happy and content while she was on the verge of a nervous breakdown.

Maybe Iron Springs hadn't failed her. Maybe she hadn't heard what it tried to tell her.

"I always thought you wanted a family," she said.

"I do."

"From what I've seen, you'll have to leave here to find a wife."

"I don't need a wife now. I have Danny."

"You won't have him if you don't find a wife."

"That's why I think you ought to marry me."

Surprise caused her to swerve in the road. "I thought you hated that idea as much as I do."

"Marriage is my only option, and you're my best choice. We can work out an equitable agreement, stay married as long as necessary, then get divorced. The whole thing won't be messed up by a tangle of emotions. It'll be pure business."

The thought of her marriage being a business deal upset her. Even though nearly all her effort so far had been poured into building her career, a successful marriage had always been her goal. Getting married in this way made her dream seem further away, less real, less attainable. No one would call her relationships with men successful, but accepting Gabe's offer made it seem like she'd given up.

On the other hand, he would lose Danny if he didn't marry someone. What kind of woman could he find to marry him by tomorrow? How would she treat Danny? Or Gabe?

Everything was up to her.

Marrying Gabe shouldn't be so hard. He would agree to her staying at her grandmother's house, even living in New York. She could come down every weekend to see Danny. She and Gabe would hardly have to see each other.

"Well, what do you say?" Gabe asked.

"I'll let you know tomorrow."

She could tell he didn't like that answer. But after being asked to marry him, in fewer than twenty-four hours, she deserved at least half of those hours to think about it.

Gabe studied Dana's profile. It seemed absolutely incredible he should be asking a woman he hadn't seen in fourteen years to marry him, a woman he barely knew, one who embodied nearly everything he distrusted. He might as well close his eyes, leap over a cliff and hope someone remembered to tie a bungie cord to his ankles. No, it was worse, like jumping out of a plane without a parachute. It could only end in disaster.

Her resemblance to Ellen frightened him. But Marshall was right. If Dana meant to shaft you, she would warn you first. She was direct, honest. Blunt, even. He hated the prospect of a second divorce. He'd promised himself if he ever remarried, it would be forever. Still, if he couldn't get Danny any other way, he'd do it. It wasn't as if he was marrying a stranger.

He wondered why he'd never realized that before. Though he hadn't seen her since she was sixteen, she'd continued to be a part of his life. Through Mattie's letters he knew about their years at that fancy New England college, their vacations in exotic places, Dana's determination to make a success of her career. Mattie had seemed almost unaware of her own great talent, but she'd chronicled Dana's success almost week by week. When she'd sent pictures of Danny, half of them included Dana.

Gabe couldn't understand Dana's almost frantic need to succeed, her willingness, like Ellen, to sacrifice nearly everything for her career. He couldn't understand how she and Mattie had stayed friends. Given the kind of life she wanted, he couldn't imagine why she concerned herself with Danny. She didn't seem to need anyone—family or friends—or need to belong anywhere. He couldn't understand such emotional isolation, her need to be so independent. Maybe she feared letting someone into her life would use up the energy she needed for her career.

Yet her decision to renovate the farmhouse caused him to wonder if she was as much of an emotional desert as she seemed. He'd seen the emotion in her eyes when she turned her car into the lane, when she saw the house, the swings, the yard. He'd also sensed she didn't want anybody with her when she entered the house. It wasn't a fancy apartment or a palatial villa on the Costa del Sol. Just a farmhouse. Still, something about those long-ago summers retained a very strong hold on her emotions.

Maybe he'd let his prejudice keep him from seeing a side of Dana that even she didn't know existed. She had insisted Mattie share her apartment. She'd been at her side through the pregnancy and Danny's birth. And during Mattie's illness, according to Mattie's last letter, Dana had virtually abandoned her job. Now she watched over Danny with the ferocity of a mother bear. Maybe Danny and Mattie had changed Dana more than either of them realized.

The more he thought about that idea, the more it intrigued him. Maybe finding the answer would help him keep his mind off her body for the few weeks they would be married—if she agreed to marry him.

He glanced to his left again. No, nothing short of unconsciousness could do that. A woman with Dana's figure should never be seen in profile. It had the power to send the juices churning through his body in a matter of seconds. And she should certainly, absolutely, positively *never* wear a short skirt when driving. A good look at those long, slim legs could send any red-blooded male over the edge. He didn't know a thing about hosiery, but Dana's made her legs look as smooth as silk. The impulse to reach out and trail his fingertips along their length was nearly impossible to resist.

Her skirt was *too* short. It ought to extend half way down her calf. Or, just to be on the safe side, down to her ankles. And it shouldn't be tight-fitting. The sight of her slim hips so cleanly outlined wasn't good for his concentration. Maybe one of those things with elastic at the waist and lots of thick, gathered material.

And that didn't take into consideration a blouse so filmy he could practically see her breasts. He knew he couldn't, but the material made him think he could. He wondered how much they paid designers to create that effect. It ought to be millions.

"Everything looks so green," Dana said.

"We've had a lot of rain."

"It ought to help prevent fires."

A hurricane couldn't have doused the fire building inside him. "We almost never have fires up here."

"I was thinking of the hay at my grandmother's farm."

"Get someone to cut it."

"I don't know anyone."

"I do."

"Will you take care of it for me?"

She turned toward him for a moment—not long enough to affect her driving, but long enough to endanger his self-control. There ought to be warning labels sown into every piece of her outfit saying *Wearer subject to attack by sex-starved males.*

Not that a man needed to be sex starved to want Dana. Even the perfume she wore tugged seductively at his senses. Half the time he couldn't catch the scent. But when he did, it acted on him like a hypnotic drug, one that a man became aware of only after it had him firmly in its coils.

Everything about this woman seemed designed to eat away at his self-control. He'd better rectify that. No matter what arrangement they reached, city-bred Dana Marsh wouldn't want anything to do with a country boy who made furniture and lived in a Podunk mountain town in Virginia.

"What time would you like to leave for Ma's house?" Gabe asked, determined to get his mind off Dana's body. She cast him a quick glance before turning her gaze back to the road. She didn't look too happy about that idea, but he hadn't expected she would.

"I'd been thinking of picking up something and spending the evening letting Danny get used to your house."

He turned to look in the back seat. Danny had gone to sleep in his car seat, his head tilted to one side. There was something about the child asleep that reached out and grabbed Gabe like nothing ever had. He couldn't decide whether it was that he was such an angelic-looking child, his complete trust that they would take care of him, or the sweet innocence of his expression. He just knew he was more determined than ever to be the one who would rear his sister's child.

"If you want to continue to be part of Danny's life, you're going to have to get to know the people in his life."

"Nobody in Iron Springs likes me."

"Maybe a few of them haven't forgotten the things

your mother said when she left—she badmouthed just about everybody and everything in Iron Springs—but the rest like you just fine.''

''No, they don't. You might not have seen it, but I felt it. I asked my grandmother about it.''

''What did she say?''

''She said to pretend it didn't exist.''

''Sounds like good advice to me.''

''It's not good enough for me now.''

''Then you'll have to figure out a way to change their minds.''

''Would marrying you do that?''

Until he married Ellen, he'd always taken belonging for granted. She looked down on everybody, and they sensed it right way.

''I don't know,'' he replied. ''I supposed you'd have to like Iron Springs, want to live here, want the people to be your friends.''

''They'd have to want me, too. I was always *that kid from New York*.''

''They probably felt you were just visiting, that you had no more intention than your mother did of having anything to do with Iron Springs after you grew up.''

''Why should they think that?''

''You were always telling us about your big plans to become a famous businesswoman and make millions of dollars.''

Back then he'd never heard of a million dollars. That figure had been a constant reminder of the great distance between their two worlds.

''Little girls always dream big.''

''A little too big for people around here.''

''It shouldn't be.'' She sounded short, a little defensive. ''You could have half a dozen millionaires in town if a few people decided to sell off a mountain or two. Even if they couldn't be used for ski slopes, they could be turned into retirement communities.''

''We don't want things to change,'' Gabe said.

Bringing that many people and that kind of business into the area would destroy most of what he loved about Iron Springs. He knew Dana wouldn't see it that way—she'd probably think it would be the salvation of the place—but she didn't see the real value, the most precious resource of Iron Springs.

The people.

''It won't matter,'' Dana said. ''If I agree to marry you, I won't be here long enough for anybody to notice.''

Gabe thought Dana was mistaken about many things. But in no instance was she further from the truth than in believing she could be anywhere without being noticed.

Dana approached Mrs. Purvis's house with trepidation. She had been the only mother to make Dana welcome when she first visited her grandmother. Even after Mattie decided to defy her father and go to college, Mrs. Purvis had never said an angry or accusing word. Still Dana felt like she was stepping into the enemy camp.

Maybe it came from her own sense of guilt over not having told Mattie's family about her illness until after her death. Coming on the heels of her father's death, Mattie felt her own impending death would be too much for her mother and Gabe. Dana thought the shock of hearing Mattie had died without their having a chance to say goodbye would be worse, but Mattie had been adamant.

''Will anybody else be here?'' Dana asked.

"I doubt it. Ma wants Danny to herself."

Mrs. Purvis opened the door before they got halfway up the sidewalk.

"I was afraid you'd be late," she said to Gabe.

"I made a point of getting here early," Gabe said as he kissed his mother's cheek. "I knew you'd be standing at the window."

But Mrs. Purvis focused her attention on Danny, who did his best to hide behind Dana.

"No need to be afraid of your old granny," she said, stooping down before him. "I intend to spoil you rotten. It'll be Gabe's job to keep you straight."

"Ma, you'll scare Dana into taking him right back to New York."

Mrs. Purvis's reaction was immediate. "She can't take him. Mattie gave him to you."

After losing a husband and a daughter within a month of each other, Dana could understand why Mrs. Purvis's emotions were brittle and close to the surface. Dana decided to do everything she could to encourage Danny to feel comfortable with his grandmother. Her own grandmother had been one of the most important influences in her life. Clearly Mrs. Purvis wanted to be just as important to Danny.

When Dana offered to help Mrs. Purvis in the kitchen, Danny followed right behind.

Mrs. Purvis got Danny's attention by offering him a bit of chicken breast. Next she gave him a slice of orange from the salad. She followed that with a dab of mashed potatoes so Danny could tell her if she'd gotten enough salt and cream to suit him. She even gave him a tiny bit of cake to make sure he liked chocolate.

"I wouldn't think of giving him very much," she said, a little guiltily Dana thought. "But I want to make sure he likes everything. The first meeting is so important.''

Dana wanted to tell her this was the second meeting, that she'd fawned over him for at least an hour earlier in the day, that Danny would eat just about anything you gave him as long as it was sweet, but she bit her tongue.

"I don't think it'll hurt him," she said. "Danny's a good eater."

"All the Purvises are. My husband put away two plates at supper until the day he died."

She looked stricken by her own words. Dana couldn't be sure whether over the loss of her husband or the reminder of his implacable attitude that had caused their separation from Mattie.

"He'll have to eat more than those little dabs if he's going to top six feet by the time he's thirteen," Gabe said. He offered Danny another piece of chicken. "It's a Purvis tradition. You'd better get started. You've only got eleven years to go."

Dana wondered if intolerance figured as a Purvis tradition, too, but she didn't say anything. The past couldn't be changed. Nothing mattered now but Danny's future.

Dana might as well not have been at the table during dinner. Mrs. Purvis spoke almost entirely to Danny. She offered him seconds and thirds on everything. It took all of Dana's diplomatic skills to keep her from feeding him until he got sick.

Gabe talked about all the things they were going to do once Danny got settled in, what he would do when he became a teenager, what he would study in college, what jobs he'd take afterward. Dana couldn't decide whether he wanted to hurry Danny's growth so he could get rid of his responsibility, or if he knew so little about little boys he could think only in terms of adult activities.

One good thing did come from the evening. Danny felt comfortable enough with Gabe to go into the den with him while Dana helped Mrs. Purvis clear away in the kitchen.

"You don't have to help me," Mrs. Purvis protested. "There's not much to do." She'd cooked enough for a dozen people. The refrigerator would be full.

"I don't mind," Dana said. "Besides, I want to give Danny a chance to get used to being with Gabe without having me around."

"He's a darling little boy. I can't believe he's my grandson."

Dana didn't know what to do when Mrs. Purvis started to tear up. She felt like a fool just standing there, but try as she might, she couldn't get past her resentment. She was sure living with a man like Mr. Purvis had to have been difficult, but she couldn't imagine herself turning her back on her only daughter no matter what the circumstances.

"I'm sorry," Mrs. Purvis said once she recovered herself. "I can't help thinking of Mattie every time I see that child." She looked straight into Dana's eyes. "I'm sure you think me an awful hypocrite for acting so upset when I didn't call or write for so many years."

Chapter Five

The shock of having her thoughts stated aloud embarrassed Dana. "I don't see how you could have done that," she finally managed to reply.

Mrs. Purvis smiled in a sad, resigned way, so gentle, so understanding, it made Dana feel awfully young. "I didn't expect you would. But many times we can't do what we want. I imagine you're starting to realize that now. You want that baby more than anything you've ever wanted in your life. You know you can't have him, but you can't make yourself let go. You'll hate it, and sometimes you'll fight it, but you'll do everything you can to make sure Danny learns to be happy here. You're a good person. You'll do what you have to do even though it hurts real bad."

Dana felt stripped, vulnerable, helpless. Mrs. Purvis had seen straight through her. Nobody else had understood a fraction of the anger she felt at having to give up Danny, of her banked rage that she and Danny were helpless pawns unable to control their own lives.

Mrs. Purvis reached out and squeezed Dana's hand. "When you get home, you're going to be lonelier than you've ever been in your life. You'll want to know all the little things about Danny, the things you always knew before but can't know now. Call me as often as you want. It won't be the same as seeing him every day, but it'll help. And you've got to come see him often. Don't let your being angry at Gabe keep you away. Danny needs you as much as ever."

Mrs. Purvis had missed nothing, yet she didn't judge Dana for any of these feelings.

Mrs. Purvis sniffed, dabbed her nose, and put her handkerchief away. "If we don't hurry and get everything put away, Danny and Gabe will be asleep on the couch before we're done."

Despite being unable to approve of what Mrs. Purvis had done, Dana had clearly misjudged Gabe's mother. She loved her family very much. Dana wondered if there might not be more to the situation than Mattie had let on.

"You two had better get out here before we find a football game," Gabe called from the den.

"You go ahead," Ms. Purvis said to Dana. "I'll be in after I put on the coffee."

Dana welcomed the relief from the emotional intensity that had sprung up between them.

When she entered the den, she found Danny and Gabe on the floor playing with a beautifully carved wooden train. She didn't have to ask if Gabe had made it. Danny jumped up, came to her, hugged her around the leg. She could see the disappointment in Gabe's eyes, but he didn't say anything.

Dana knelt on the floor, pulled Danny down with her. "Did Gabe show you how to run the train?"

"Yes."

"Show me."

Danny took hold of the engine and pulled the train in a circle around him as he pivoted on his hands and knees. He tried to make the sounds of the train whistle and the chug-chug of the steam locomotive, but he only succeeded in spraying the train.

"You got things a little wet," Dana said.

"Gabe says I slobber."

She could tell Danny didn't like that. "I'll bet Gabe can't sound like a train without slobbering. I know I can't."

"Can you?" Danny asked Gabe.

"Let's see," Gabe replied.

Much to Dana's relief, Gabe managed to slobber just as much as Danny. He had a lot to learn about children, but he was a quick study. Leaving Danny with Gabe might not be so bad if she had time to help them both make the transition.

"You slobbered," Danny crowed.

"He sure did," Dana said. "And he's a big people."

"Big people don't slobber?" Danny asked.

"They try not to," Dana said.

Danny took the train from Gabe. He pulled it in a circle and made his whoo-whoo sound.

"Danny no slobber," he said proudly. Then he pointed at Gabe. "Gabe slobber."

"You're a competitive little thing," Gabe said. "At two, conquering slobber. At twenty-two, the world."

Dana got the feeling Gabe didn't approve. "He's just trying to be grown-up," she explained. "Every child tries to imitate adults."

"He ought to stay a kid as long as he can."

"We never learn that until it's too late."

"I won't have you two getting philosophical," Mrs. Purvis said as she entered the room carrying a large serving tray on which sat three mugs of coffee, the sippy cup Dana had brought for Danny and a plate of oatmeal raisin cookies.

"Ma, we're still full from dinner," Gabe protested.

"Cookies?" Danny asked.

"You can have one," Dana said. She chuckled in spite of herself. "And if you still have room after that, you can have another."

Danny chose the biggest cookie on the plate.

"Don't drop crumbs on the rug," Dana warned.

"Let him enjoy his cookie," Mrs. Purvis said. "I can vacuum after he leaves."

"I have an idea," Gabe said. "Let's load some cookies on the train. That way Grandma and Dana won't eat them all."

Danny promptly filled both hands with cookies and put them on the train. He went back for a second load.

"We'd better take our cookies and run before Dana makes us give them back," Gabe said.

Gabe put a few more cookies on the train, balanced the sippy cup on top of a cattle car and drove the train out of the den into the kitchen. Danny followed happily.

"They can make all the mess they want in there," Mrs. Purvis said. She took an album off the shelf and settled down in the sofa. "I want to show you something," she said. She opened the album to some pictures of Dana and Mattie in their first dormitory room.

"Where did you get these?" Dana asked.

"Mattie sent them."

"But I thought..." She let that sentence die away unfinished.

"She said her father would open the mail," Mrs. Purvis finished for her. "She sent them to Hannah. She gave them to Gabe, and he gave them to me."

"Why didn't either one of you call?"

"That was *her* restriction. She knew it would have made her father angry."

"When did she say all this?"

"When Gabe went to see her."

"When? I never knew."

"He tried to convince Mattie to come home three times, once in college, once in Atlanta and the last time when she was living with you. He offered to let her live in his house, but she said she wasn't going to change and neither would her father."

Dana couldn't believe Mattie hadn't told her about the visits, the pictures, Gabe's offer. Maybe she hadn't wanted Dana to get caught up in her family troubles. Maybe she thought Dana already had enough pressure on her at work. Dana felt hurt nonetheless. She thought she and Mattie had shared everything.

Mrs. Purvis quickly flipped through pictures of their college years to pictures of Mattie's apartment in Atlanta. She paused at one of Mattie and an extremely handsome older man. "Is that Danny's father?" she asked.

Dana didn't know what she could do but answer the question. "Yes."

"What's he like?"

Dana hesitated, not knowing what to say.

"I can see he's very handsome," Mrs. Purvis said. "Quite charming, I expect."

"Very."

"I suppose that's what fooled Mattie."

Dana felt uneasy about revealing Mattie's secrets, but she wanted to offer Mrs. Purvis some explanation.

"He pursued Mattie, made a lot of promises, kept after her until she gave in. But when she got pregnant, everything changed. He demanded that she get rid of the baby. When she refused, he left her."

"He should have known Mattie would never do that."

"He would have if he'd been the kind of man who could love Mattie as much as she loved him."

"Her father wanted her to come home, have the baby and give it up for adoption."

"Mattie couldn't do that, either."

"Her father could never understand. It made him unable to forgive her."

She paused for a moment, reliving something in her mind, then turned until she found the first pictures of Danny. "She sent me pictures of him every month. I used to go to Gabe's house to look at them. But pictures aren't enough. I wanted somebody to tell me about all the things pictures can't tell. Will you do that?"

"I'll be glad to."

Dana thought talking about the pictures would make her sad, but Mrs. Purvis's eagerness to feel closer to her daughter heightened Dana's pleasure in revisiting those cherished memories.

At first, Dana could hear Gabe and Danny in the kitchen, but she gradually became so wrapped up in the pictures she was surprised when Gabe came in carrying a very sleepy Danny.

"It's time to put him to bed."

"I not sleepy," Danny protested as he rubbed his eyes.

"Of course you're not," Gabe said, "but Dana is. We have to put her to bed."

"Not put Danie to bed. She too big."

"I'll help, okay?"

"Okay." His eyes were only half open.

"I didn't realize it was so late," Dana said, getting to her feet.

"It's my fault," Mrs. Purvis said.

"It's been a long day," Dana said. "The trip wore him out. Thanks for the dinner. I'll carry him."

"He's fine where he is," Gabe replied.

Danny fell asleep on Gabe's shoulder before they reached the front door. Mrs. Purvis kissed him good-night twice. Danny smiled without opening his eyes.

"It was very nice of your mother to invite us to dinner," Dana said as they headed toward Gabe's house.

"What's wrong?" Gabe asked.

"What do you mean?"

"You're upset."

Looking at the pictures and talking about Mattie and Danny had temporarily distracted her thoughts, but Dana was angry. "Why should I be upset?"

"I don't know, but you sound like you're about ready to bite nails. Ma didn't say anything to upset you, did she? She's been worried sick about making a good impression on you and Danny."

"Your mother's a lovely woman. She obviously adores Danny. The worst thing she'll do is spoil him."

"So I'm the one you're mad at. What have I done this time?"

She couldn't see any point in bringing it up. Knowing why he did it—if he could possibly offer a reason that wouldn't make her even more angry—wouldn't change anything.

"It's nothing."

He settled Danny more comfortably on his shoulder. "If you get your insides in this kind of knot over nothing, you must go over the edge when you have a real problem. Mattie said you were always stressed out."

"It's nice to know you and Mattie talked about me so often."

This conversation hadn't gone at all the way she wanted. Instead of putting all thought of his avoiding her out of her mind, she had grown angrier than ever. How dare he talk about her behind her back.

"If you don't get it out, you're going to burst wide open."

She hesitated.

"I thought you were a woman of action. Maybe that's why things aren't going so well with your job."

"Why did you avoid me when you came to New York?" she burst out. "Mattie didn't say a word. Was that your doing?"

"I assume Ma told you about that."

"She had to have some explanation for all those pictures."

"Mattie sent them because I asked her to."

"Why did you time your visits so you wouldn't see me?"

"I wanted to make sure Mattie was doing what she wanted, not what you wanted for her."

Dana nearly exploded. "I never strong-armed Mattie into anything. I bent over backward to make sure she could do what she wanted, not what her family thought she ought to do."

"I know. Mattie told me. She made it clear she liked her work and had no intentions of coming home. She said I owed you an apology. So I'm offering it now. I apologize for thinking you attempted to influence what Mattie did or thought.''

That took the wind out of her sails and left her practically in shock.

''So why did you avoid me?'' It wasn't what she wanted to ask, but it probably wasn't important now.

''I didn't want you working your wiles on me.''

That surprised a laugh out of her. ''When could I ever work my wiles on you? You're totally impervious to any charm, wiles or mediocre attributes Mother Nature gave me.''

Now Gabe laughed. ''Cautious. Perhaps living in mortal fear, but never impervious. You can do almost as much damage with one of your smiles as Marshall could do if he got his hands on a shotgun. And that doesn't begin to cover what happens to my temperature when I see you wearing a short skirt.

Dana didn't know if she could absorb any more shocks in one evening. She'd thought Gabe was completely unaware of her as a woman, that he believed her off base at nearly every turn, that he never considered her important enough to do more than feed her ice cream from time to time. To have him apologize and say he'd found her attractive put her into emotional overload.

''You managed to hide it quite well.''

''It's not hard when I haven't seen you in fourteen years.''

Did he mean he'd thought about her at any time during those years? Had he looked at the pictures for any reason other than Mattie and Danny? ''It's probably just as well we didn't meet,'' she said.

''Probably.''

Yet the silence that hung between them declared something had been left unsaid.

"You think I should have stood up for Mattie, don't you?" Gabe asked.

She always had. "I never understood why you didn't."

"Mattie asked me not to. She said she knew Pa would never change his mind. He just wasn't made that way. She said she didn't want what she did to affect me or Ma. She knew if Ma and I tried to make Pa understand, it would have caused even more trouble. She insisted on being the only one to take blame for what happened."

That sounded exactly like Mattie, always ready to take more than her share of responsibility, anxious to shield everyone else. "Still—"

"Mattie and Pa never got along because they were too much alike, one just as stubborn as the other. I knew it wouldn't do any good. Neither would change their mind."

Dana wasn't sure she agreed with Gabe, but despite twenty-five years of being the best of friends, Mattie hadn't told her everything. In fact, she had left out some very important details. She could only guess how much more Mattie had kept from her.

"You don't agree with me, do you?" Gabe asked.

She shrugged.

"You were her best friend, but I was her brother. I saw her in ways you never could."

Dana wanted to argue with him, but she'd seen Mattie and her father together very few times. She had avoided Mr. Purvis. She had been a little afraid of him as a child.

She could easily see how a woman who loved her husband and prized her family would feel caught between her husband and a rebellious child, unable to openly sympathize with one without alienating the other.

She could also see why, if forced to choose, Mrs. Purvis would have chosen to preserve her marriage.

"I'm glad she sent those pictures to your mother," Dana said. "She enjoyed them so much. She must have had great fun putting them in the albums."

"I put them in the albums," Gabe said. "I didn't always agree with what Mattie did—I rarely agreed with the way she chose to do it—but I loved my sister. Her virtually abandoning the family was the worst thing that ever happened to us."

"Worse than your divorce?" Dana was mortified to hear herself voice that question. She'd meant it to be a thought.

"My marriage was my mistake," Gabe said. "Afterward, things went back to being pretty much as they always were. Mattie left a hole in the family that never got filled."

Dana wanted to ask him how anything could ever be the same after a divorce, but they'd reached Gabe's house. She was astonished when he simply opened the door. He hadn't locked his house.

"Could you turn on the light?" he said. "I don't want to wake Danny."

She couldn't figure out how her cutting on the light would help until she saw Gabe using his hand to shield Danny's eyes from the light.

"I've got to undress him," Dana said.

"Can't we put him in bed in his clothes?"

"No." Only a man would ask a question like that. She followed Gabe up the wide staircase. "Don't take him in his bedroom."

"Why not?"

"I don't want him to wake up and find himself alone in a strange house. I'll let him sleep with me."

"Do you think that's wise?"

"It's better than having him wake up and be frightened."

"I guess it won't be too bad. You won't be here very long."

His words brought back the one fact above all others she'd been trying to forget. Being in Iron Springs made it easy to feel New York and the rest of the world were far away, that nothing could ever penetrate these mountains to harm her. Yet Iron Springs had hurt her far more than New York ever could.

She shoved all that from her mind. "If you'll help me, maybe we can get him into his pajamas without waking him."

Gabe's gentleness surprised her. She guessed she thought big men of rough manners, decided opinions, and firmly held beliefs lacked a gentle side altogether. That might be true of others, but not Gabe. He laid Danny down on the bed without causing an eyelid to flicker, untied and removed Danny's shoes while Dana took off his shirt. Gabe helped her with the pants. He yielded to Dana when it came time to change his diaper, but Dana had no doubt he'd know how to do it next time.

"You're going to put him in those?" Gabe asked when Dana pulled out a pair of pajamas decorated with teddy bears.

"What's wrong with them?" she hissed.

"I'll tell you tomorrow," he said.

He frowned so the whole time he helped her put them on, she knew she'd contravened one of those mysterious codes only men understood. She still doubted the wisdom of Mattie's insisting Danny be reared by a man, but she no longer doubted there were certain areas of the male psyche no female could hope to fathom.

You didn't have to be female to know Danny looked perfectly adorable in sleep. Dana had often wondered what made people—but especially babies—look so irresistible in sleep. Even rumpled, with hair in their faces, all the innocence and sweetness seemed to come to the surface during slumber.

"He's a real cute kid, isn't he?"

Gabe's whispered voice disturbed her thoughts.

"Yes, he is."

"He looks just like Mattie."

"Mattie said she'd never been that adorable."

"She was. Dad used to dote on her. I think that's what made it so hard for him to accept what happened later."

Leave it to a man to find a way destroy a tender moment. "We'd better leave before we wake him up."

Gabe moved to the doorway. "Do you know where everything is?"

She could tell he didn't want her in his house. She supposed she couldn't blame him. After all, she had invited herself.

"I've got everything I need in my suitcase."

"I mean in the kitchen. You'll need to fix Danny's breakfast."

She hadn't thought that far ahead. "Do you have milk?"

"Yes."

"I have Danny's cereal. We'll be fine." They hadn't moved from the doorway. It made Dana nervous. She wanted Gabe to leave. She headed down the stairs, hoping he would follow. He did.

"Do you need anything from the car?" he asked when they reached the bottom.

"No." She walked toward the front door. She wondered if he'd be comfortable at his mother's. She knew Mrs. Purvis would try to mother him. Gabe didn't look like the kind of man to enjoy that.

"You do have a key for the front door, don't you?" she asked, remembering he hadn't locked it.

"You don't need to lock the door."

"Probably not, but I'm not used to sleeping with unlocked doors. I wouldn't get a wink of sleep."

"The key's in the door. But I wish you could trust the townspeople."

"Why?"

"Because I want you to marry me so I can keep Danny."

Chapter Six

At least he had the decency not to pretend he'd fallen in love with her honey-brown hair, brown eyes or fabulous figure. He just wanted Danny, and he'd do anything he must to keep him. She should have been relieved he didn't pretend feelings he couldn't possibly have. But appreciating his honesty did nothing to loosen the double knot that had formed in her stomach.

"I'll have to think about it."

"Marshall said we didn't have much time."

"We have until tomorrow." She wondered if her voice sounded a little desperate to him. That's how she felt, pressured on all sides by decisions she didn't want to make, *couldn't* make, on the spur of the moment.

"We'd have to get married tomorrow. I have to know tonight so I can make the arrangements."

She didn't want an explanation. It would just make

the pressure worse. "We haven't talked about any-thing."

"What do you need to know beyond the fact that you can get a divorce the minute I get custody of Danny?"

"All kinds of things," she said, feeling as desperate as she sounded. "We haven't worked out the living arrangements."

"We'll sleep in separate bedrooms."

"People will ask questions."

"We'll think of something to tell them."

"I still don't know. I—"

"I'll put a lock on your door if it'll make you feel better."

"I trust you." She would never agree to marry him if she didn't trust him, not even for a few weeks.

"Good, that's taken care of. I'll sign any kind of pre-nuptial agreement you want."

"What for?"

"So I won't have a claim on your money. You'll be abandoning Danny and me. That would give me grounds to take you for all you're worth."

She'd never thought of a prenuptial agreement. Gabe would never try to take her family's money. He was too proud.

"You can make as many trips to New York as you like."

"I don't imagine my being away a lot would make a very good impression on the judge."

"He wouldn't have to know."

"Sooner or later everybody knows everything in a place like this."

"He doesn't live in Iron Springs."

"He'd find out anyway."

"Look, Dana," he said when she didn't respond immediately, "I'll do anything you want, sign any paper, agree to any conditions."

"Think of the women who'd give everything they own for a proposal like that."

"I doubt they'd be too pleased with the divorce tacked on at the end," Gabe said.

He didn't have to make fun of her just because she'd tried to keep things from becoming unbearably tense.

"You're probably encouraging me to go back to New York because you can't stand the thought of me in your house."

"I hardly know you. But even if I disliked you, I'd still ask you to marry me. Danny is all the family Ma and I have left. I'll do anything to keep him."

Dana didn't know why Gabe's answer didn't soothe her anxiety. He'd said exactly what she wanted him to say. He'd promised to do everything he could to make the situation as easy for her as possible. She couldn't ask any more of a man who must be going through agonies to make the offer at all.

"I'll let you know first thing in the morning," she said. "I know you want an answer right now, but I'll be more clearheaded after a good night's sleep."

But when Gabe had made his final plea, gathered what he needed for the night, and she'd locked the front door behind him, she felt too keyed up to sleep. The mere thought of being married to Gabe had set every nerve in her body on edge. Living in the same house, doing things together, *acting like a married couple,* filled her mind with vivid images she couldn't have imagined only a few hours ago.

The magnetism she'd felt the moment she stepped into Marshall's kitchen had continued to grow until it felt like a physical force acting on her body. Looking at him and being in the same room with him had been difficult. Being alone in the car and at the farm had heightened the feeling. It had dissipated only slightly at his mother's. It intensified again on the walk home, flared when he helped her put Danny to bed, and nearly consumed her when he asked her to marry him.

She couldn't understand it. If she hadn't known better, she'd have said she was attracted to him again, that she actually liked him, that she could *enjoy* being married to him.

Nothing could be further from the truth. She could find only two possible explanations. Maybe Gabe was too handsome, too overwhelmingly masculine, too much the perfect realization of a woman's dream for Dana *not* to be attracted to him.

On the other hand, it could simply be the resurrection of her youthful feelings. She'd been wildly in love with him until that fateful evening. Maybe, even though her mind and emotional maturity had traveled a long distance since that day, her physical attraction to him had become frozen in time. Maybe a small part of her had stayed that teenage girl worshiping the older man she'd always dreamed of marrying.

In that case, marrying him would be a good thing. She'd be around Gabe long enough to give her physical attraction time to shift from the past into the present. If he was just too good looking to be ignored no matter what her mental, emotional or physical state, she'd just have to endure it. She'd done it in business situations. She could do it here.

But she had never been expected to live in the man's house.

She turned away from the front door and came face-to-face with Gabe's grandfather clock. She couldn't possible look at that beautifully finished wood, the intricate carving, without thinking of Gabe. It wouldn't do any good to turn her head. Everywhere she looked her gaze fell on his work, all of it a testament to craftsmanship that couldn't be ignored. But it wasn't the skill that drew her, it was the soul of the craftsman evident in each piece of work, the way a wood's texture and color seemed to have been specifically chosen for a particular design, a particular piece, to stand in a particular place. Decorative detail never overshadowed the simple beauty of material or function.

Dana had worked with masterpieces of craftsmanship far too long to fail to see flashes of genius in Gabe's work, sparks that testified to the existence of a part of Gabe she'd never seen. Any man who could lavish such care and attention on a piece of wood, should be able to create a masterpiece of love when it came to a woman.

She shivered. Being in his house was causing her to think all kinds of crazy thoughts. She ought to get out of Iron Springs before she started doing something really crazy.

Like forgetting Gabe had proved no one could love her for herself, just what she appeared to be.

Yet she felt drawn to the big, spacious house. It had been built more than fifty years earlier by local craftsmen from local lumber without benefit of an architect's plans. Its fourteen-foot ceilings, glass above doors, plaster molding, and central hall from front to back stamped it as belonging to another era. Dana couldn't imagine what it would be like to live here. Surely it would be like playacting, stepping into a past that hadn't existed for years.

Then she remembered her summers with her grandmother, days spent doing various chores, hours spent visiting, quiet evenings after dinner spent on the porch swinging and talking until time to go to bed. Suddenly, it didn't see quite so impossible. She remembered how happy she'd been, how much her grandmother loved Iron Springs. It was a different way of living, one that probably required a very different set of priorities from the ones necessary for surviving in the cutthroat business of high-priced antiques, but there were parts of it that were very attractive, very seductive. She might tire of it after a short while, but it would be a nice change.

What was she thinking! She couldn't possibly like living in Iron Springs. She had to be mentally exhausted. There could be no other reason for her thinking such mad thoughts. Next she'd be thinking she was marrying Gabe because he loved her for the person she was, not her money, looks or success. It wouldn't happen. He'd made that very clear fourteen years ago.

But when she went into the living room to turn off the light, her gaze fell on an open photo album. The first picture that caught her attention was one of her and Mattie when they were eight and Gabe had taken them swimming in a nearby lake. They stood clutching black inner tubes, clad in those terrible one-piece bathing suits all little girls wore. Gabe had devoted the whole afternoon to them, making every other female in sight jealous. Even at fourteen, Gabe's good looks made women take notice. He'd been kind and attentive, and Dana had had a wonderful time.

She wondered if he'd changed as much as it seemed. She told herself that had nothing to do with her decision whether or not to marry him. If she did, she would do so for one reason only—to protect Danny from a father who wanted him only because of his gender.

Still Dana had the distinct feeling being married to

Gabe, even for only a few weeks, could be dangerous. If she didn't exercise great care, she might do something foolish like start thinking of him as a hero again.

She closed the album, turned off the light and left the room. Tomorrow would be a new day. And before it got very old, she'd have to decide whether to marry Gabe. She feared trying to make that decision would keep her awake most of the night.

Gabe stared into the mirror at his own bleary-eyed reflection. He looked like something out of a horror movie. He had spent the whole night tossing and turning in the bed he'd slept in as a teenager. He fought off a nearly overwhelming urge to crawl back into bed and forget the troubles that had descended on him when a certain forest-green Jaguar rolled into town.

"You up, Gabe?" his mother called.

She knew he was up. You could hear the water running in the pipes all over the house. "Yeah, Ma, I'm up."

"What do you want for breakfast?"

His mother was a morning person. She bubbled over with good cheer from the moment she opened her eyes. It practically set Gabe's teeth on edge. "I don't want anything." He'd eaten too much last night. His mouth felt like cotton and tasted a lot worse, and he was far too grumpy to make polite conversation.

"You have to eat. You can't go to the shop on an empty stomach."

"Yes, I can, Ma." He'd stopped eating breakfast after his divorce.

"It's not good for you."

"You've been telling me that for years."

"It's still the truth."

"I don't want anything. I've got to see Dana."

"No need to rush. She's not going anywhere."

She couldn't understand because she didn't know what was as stake. But he could see no point in worrying her when she couldn't do anything about it. He had to solve this problem alone.

"I'll tell you what we decide," he said.

"I don't need to know. I'm not nosy."

Most mothers would want to know if their only son planned to get married later that day.

"You'll want to know about Danny." He knew he had her there. She'd spent nearly an hour talking about Danny after he got back to the house last night.

"I'll be back shortly," he said. "If you're already at work, I'll drop by."

"This is Saturday. I don't go to work."

Which just went to show how rattled he'd been since Dana arrived. "Sorry. I forgot."

He headed for the front door, his mother trailing behind. "Maybe Dana would bring Danny over for breakfast. I'm sure he likes pancakes."

"She's been taking care of him for a long time. I'm sure she's got a routine."

"She's so good with Danny," his mother said. "She was always a sweet child even though she could never sit still, but I never expected her to take such good care of Danny. He's going to miss her a lot." Then she added, almost as an afterthought, "But not as much as she's going to miss him."

Gabe had been trying to convince himself Dana was clinging to Danny out of habit, that she'd soon be ready to go back to her normal way of life. "You think she's going to miss him that much?" he asked.

"She loves him like he's her own child. It's going to break her heart to give him up."

"There's no other way."

"I realize that, but it's not going to change the hurt."

Now he felt guilty for wanting Dana to go back to New York. "Maybe we can think of something," he said.

"What?"

Leave it to his mother to pin him down immediately. "I don't know. I've got to go. I'll be back in a little while."

The morning air was thick and muggy. Must have been a shower somewhere in the valley. The atmosphere matched Gabe's mood. He hadn't been able to think of any more reasons to convince Dana to marry him. Promising to let her see Danny whenever she wanted—even sending him to New York for visits—wouldn't bring her around. She knew she could come down anytime she wanted. He didn't want to mention that she owed it to Mattie's memory. That would be unfair. Besides, she already knew that.

Searching for ways to convince Dana to marry him wasn't the only thing that had kept him awake, staring wide-eyed at the ceiling long after midnight. The idea of being married to Dana, even a pretend marriage, had set him in a uproar.

He'd never denied Dana's attractiveness. He'd conceded that every time he'd seen her over the summers she'd spent in Iron Springs. But he'd never thought of much beyond that. She was his little sister's best friend. Back then six years seemed like a yawning chasm. Even after Dana declared she loved him, begged him to wait for her, he hadn't taken her feelings seriously. She was just a rich, overindulged young girl with a crush on an older guy. She always talked about her rich friends, the schools she attended, her trips all over the world, how she planned to be such a great success everybody in New York would know her name. They had nothing in common, and he'd told her so.

Now her devotion to Danny had forced him to reconsider. At least, he *thought* that was the reason for the strong attraction that had sprung up almost the moment he set eyes on her. The steady stream of pictures Mattie had sent him over the years had enabled Gabe to follow Dana's transformation from a pretty girl into a mature, sensual woman. He would be lying to himself if he didn't admit he'd occasionally fantasized about what it would have been like if he'd married Dana instead of Ellen. He'd had some pretty hot dreams.

But that's all they were. And they came crashing down every time he remembered the differences that separated them—money, social position and ambition, just to name a few.

Still, desire had flared up the minute she'd walked into Marshall's kitchen. When they'd been in the car together he'd almost had to grab the door handle to keep from touching her. If he couldn't control himself during a short drive, how would he survive being married to her, living in the same house, being around her several hours a day for as much as *two or three months?*

Despite her independence and her annoying habit of arguing with nearly every word that came out of his mouth, she was vital, energetic and seductively feminine. He felt like a weak-willed idiot, a teenager being jerked around by runaway hormones, but he couldn't stop it.

He had to get himself under control. Only the threat of losing Danny had forced Dana to consider marrying him. Only the promise he would leave her completely alone, wouldn't do anything to hinder her divorce, had induced her even to consider such a drastic step. He would have to control his reaction to her. If she had any idea of the thoughts that went through his mind, she'd fire up that Jaguar and be on I-81 in ten minutes. He would control himself because he must to keep Danny. His feelings didn't matter to anyone but himself.

He walked up the steps to the screened-in back porch of his house and reached for the door handle.

The door didn't open. She had latched the door. That never happened in Iron Springs. It showed him even more clearly how much they were unalike. Feeling decidedly off balance, he banged on the door with his fist. He didn't have a doorbell. He never needed one.

Dana peered through the kitchen window. With Danny perched on her hip, she hurried out to unlatch the screen. "What are you doing here?" she asked as he entered the porch.

"It's my house." He had started off on the wrong foot. He wouldn't convince her to marry him by acting like this. "I came to see how you were doing," he said. "Did you sleep well? Did you find something for breakfast?"

It wasn't fair. She looked delicious this early in the morning. She wore a halter top, skimpy shorts and nothing else. Even her feet were bare. He'd never realized how sexy feet could be. Five seconds on the porch, and his temperature had started to rise. Not a good sign.

"We've just found our way to the kitchen," Dana said. "Come on in." She issued the invitation with obvious reluctance.

Dana wasn't really ready to face Gabe, but in a way she was glad to see him. She certainly hadn't expected

him to neglect his work to come see how she was doing.
But then, that wasn't really why he came. He'd come to
see if she'd agree to marry him, if she'd help him keep
Danny.

"What are you fixing?" Gabe asked.

"Danny has his own cereal. I have coffee."

"Don't you eat real food?"

"I'm not hungry in the morning. I don't wake up easily."

"You look wide awake to me."

She wasn't certain how he meant that, but the way his
gaze kept straying over her body made her wish she'd
put on something that covered a little more. She wasn't
accustomed to being around a man in the morning.
"You have to be, when you have a child to take care
of," she said.

"You look awake enough to eat some bacon and
eggs."

She smiled. "Good old country food."

"Naw, this is practically fast food." He opened the
refrigerator, took things out and put them on the counter.
"If we were sitting down to breakfast at my grandmother's house, we'd have ham, sausage, maybe a pork-
chop or two, probably some beef and gravy, eggs, grits,
biscuits slathered in butter and dripping with jam, big
glasses of milk and pots of hot coffee."

"Stop. I feel my arteries clogging just talking about
it."

"My grandparents are still alive," Gabe said, "and
still eating the same foods." He found a tray, laid six
strips of bacon on it, covered it with a paper towel, and
put it in the microwave.

"I can't believe you actually own a microwave,"
Dana said.

"Even Iron Springs is aware we're in the twentieth century."

She hadn't meant it that way. While she stirred Danny's oatmeal to cool it sufficiently for him to eat, Gabe broke several eggs into a bowl and whisked them. He found a frying pan, sprayed it to keep the eggs from sticking, put it on the burner to get hot. Meanwhile, he put bread in the toaster, set out butter and jam.

While he cooked, she set the table in between feeding Danny spoonfuls of his favorite blueberry flavored oatmeal. She usually let him feed himself, but he hadn't learned to handle the spoon very well, or find his mouth on the first try, and she didn't want to mess up Gabe's kitchen.

It seemed no time at all before Gabe had breakfast on the table.

"You did that very quickly," she said, pouring her coffee, the one thing she'd been allowed to do.

"I don't usually eat breakfast, but I still remember how to fix it."

She couldn't picture Gabe in the kitchen, not even to fix toast.

"How about some scrambled eggs?" Gabe said to Danny. "You're young enough to eat concentrated protein."

Gabe held out some eggs on a fork, and Danny opened his mouth. The child would eat virtually anything.

"Good, isn't it?" Gabe said. "Want some more?"

Danny nodded. Dana watched Danny wolf down eggs and tiny bits of bacon as if he hadn't already had his usual breakfast. She buttered some toast, finally gave in and took a serving of eggs and one piece of bacon. She grinned when she took her first bite. Gabe had put cheddar cheese in the eggs. No wonder Danny was eating like a little pig. He loved cheese.

Much to her surprise, Dana realized they were fixing and eating breakfast like an old married couple. Gabe even fed Danny, something all pediatricians urged fathers to do. According to doctors, it helped cement the bond between them. If Gabe wanted to find a way to win Danny's affections, he couldn't have found a better way than food. Besides, the eggs and bacon were very good. She didn't know if she could give the credit to Gabe's cooking, but she actually had an appetite.

"If things could go this smoothly all the time, I wouldn't mind being married to you."

Chapter Seven

The words popped out before she even thought. The stunned look on Gabe's face told her she'd surprised him as much as herself. "I mean it wouldn't be so bad *having* to be married to you for a couple of months."

He sighed and seemed to relax. A slow smile spread over his face. "I hoped you'd made up your mind to do it, for Danny's sake."

She had made it and unmade it a dozen times during the night, but she got cold feet every time she thought of it. And the smile on Gabe's lips right now was a perfect example of the danger he posed. If he smiled at her like that very often, she didn't know how long she could keep herself under control.

"I do have some conditions," she forced herself to say before she could change her mind.

"Anything you want."

"You'd better hear them first."

"I trust you."

That was more than she could say for herself. She wondered why a woman who didn't *want* to be captivated could be completely enthralled against her will. It didn't seem fair. It certainly didn't seem sensible. And she'd been extremely sensible for years.

"You already mentioned separate bedrooms and my freedom to come and go as I please."

He nodded.

"I still get to make most of the decisions concerning Danny. You don't know him yet," she said before he could argue. "I know you play with him on the kitchen floor and you've shamelessly stuffed him with eggs and bacon, but he still needs me as an anchor."

"Then you've got to agree to help him shift his anchor."

"Fair enough. I'll start writing down all the things you need to know about him. I'm bound to forget something, so don't hesitate to call me."

"Wouldn't it be quicker to ask someone here?"

"You can ask anybody you want, but you've got to call me. I don't care what time it is. I'll give you my home, work and cell phone numbers. I don't want to come for a visit and find he's been sick and I didn't know about it."

"Are you sure knowing he's sick won't worry you too much?"

"No, because I'll be here in two hours." The child would think she didn't love him any more if he was sick, hurt, or suffering and she wasn't with him. "I also want unlimited visits. I want to come anytime and stay as long as I can. I'll be here every birthday, vacation and holiday. I want to know every time there's something special, like he's in a school play or a Christmas pageant, his first soccer game—all those things.''

''You sure you don't want us to move to New York?''

She knew Gabe thought he was making a harmless joke, but if he had any idea how much she wanted Danny where she could see him every day, hug him, kiss him, love him, he wouldn't say things like that.

''I want pictures at least once a week,'' she added, ''lots of them. You said they were important to you and your mother, so you'll understand why they're important to me.''

She had to stop. The lump in her throat wouldn't allow more words to pass. She turned so she could brush away a tear without Gabe knowing. Men accused women of using tears as a weapon to get what they wanted. They couldn't seem to understand it was also an involuntary reaction to losing something precious.

''Anything else?'' Gabe asked.

''No. That's it for me.''

''I don't see any problem with any of that.''

''Good. What about you?''

''Until I win official custody, I need you to stay in Iron Springs as much as you can, doing everything you can to appear like a normal wife.''

''What did you think I'd do?''

''How can I tell? I don't know how long you can stay away from your job. You don't like Iron Springs. Your family, friends and all the things you like to do are back in New York. It would be easy to leave after the wedding and not come back.''

''I wouldn't have agreed to any of this if I weren't prepared to make the marriage look real,'' she said, irritated he would think her so irresponsible. ''I do like Iron Springs. I just don't think the people here like me.''

"They do. They just haven't had a chance to show it yet."

She decided not to argue. They'd never agree. "I think it'll be best if we don't tell anybody why we're getting married."

"I won't tell anybody but Ma."

"Not even her."

That upset him. "Why not?"

"Because your mother is too sweet and honest to carry this off if she knew the truth. She'd probably burst into tears every time she saw me." She could tell by the heavy frown he didn't like her analysis of the situation. "I'm not going to tell my parents, either."

"I should hope not. They'd have you in a psychiatric hospital within twenty-four hours, that is if they could get here that quickly from wherever they are now."

Dana bridled but said nothing. Her father had flown to Malaysia on business, and her mother was relaxing at a private resort in Switzerland.

"I still insist we tell no one," Dana said.

Gabe sighed his acceptance. "Okay, but you'll have to help me explain to Ma afterward."

"You'll do just fine by yourself. There's not a woman alive you can't twist around your fingers."

"You."

"You've talked me into marrying you. I consider that enough twisting."

"But it's only for a couple of months."

"As if you'd want to be married to me for the rest of your life."

His frozen expression confirmed her conviction he'd rather move to the center of Manhattan than cohabit with her for as much as a week. It wasn't very flattering, but she hadn't expected anything else. Didn't want it. He was an unfeeling boob, even if he did manage to act human from time to time. Still, considering her lack of success with men, it would be nice to have at least one man panting after her. He wasn't her ideal man—he'd never look right living in a Dutch Colonial in Chappaqua—though in an Iron Springs sort of way, he wasn't a bad substitute.

"So...I guess that's it," she said pleasantly surprised they'd been able to settle things so quickly. She guessed relief over how well negotiations had gone accounted for her now friendly feelings toward Gabe. He could be decent when he tried, at least when he wanted something badly enough to try. Maybe that was too harsh. He didn't understand her at all, but he had let her do pretty much what she wanted when it came to Danny.

She couldn't deny that rankled. Just once she'd like him to do something to please her. Not Danny, not anybody else. Just her.

"We've got to be at the church by noon," Gabe said. "You don't have to wear anything fancy. There won't be anybody there but the preacher, Marshall and Ma."

"What are you talking about?" Only shock caused her to ask such a stupid question. He must have taken it for granted she'd marry him. He had everything already set up.

"No point in getting mad," he said, calmly forestalling her outburst. "I could have canceled the arrangements if you refused, but if we're going to get married by high noon, I had to get things organized in case you said yes. Marshall had things to do to get a licence and arrange for blood tests."

That left Dana with nothing to say. His reasons were logical and justifiable. All the more reason she wanted to hit him. Where did he get off being rational when she felt she'd been living in a fifth dimension for the past month?

"I don't want a reception," she said, unable to think of any other way to show her anger at his making all the arrangements without consulting her.

"There won't be one."

"And there won't be a honeymoon trip."

"Naturally. I expect I'll be tied up trying to convince that lawyer he's come here on a wild-goose chase."

He would convince the lawyer, not *they*. Just like a man to assume he would be the one to do anything important.

"What will you do about a ring?"

"We can use Ellen's. She was kind enough to throw it at me just before she walked out."

She'd like to throw it at him, too. "I'll be sure to give it back."

"You can do anything you like with it. I'd forgotten I had it."

She didn't believe that.

"Anything else?" he asked.

"No." She couldn't think of any reason to postpone this nightmare. Since she had agreed to go through with it, the sooner the better.

Gabe stood. "See you later, little fella," he said to Danny. "I'm off to break the news to your grandmother. I hope she will have regained consciousness in time for the wedding."

"If she's going to object that much—"

"Don't get your back up," Gabe said. "She's been trying for years to get me to remarry. She won't be able to decide whether she's more thrilled I've finally done it or surprised it happened so quickly. Either way, once she gets over the shock, she'll be delighted. You're about to become a saint.''

''Why, for heaven's sake?''

''You're the female who's going to keep the Purvis lineage from withering on the vine.''

''What's she going to say when she learns the truth?''

Gabe sobered. ''I don't know. If it weren't for Danny, I'd never consider doing anything like this to her.''

Dana didn't understand why that should make her feel like some sort of sleazy female. She had placed her reputation on the line, too. What had seemed only difficult and objectionable a short while ago now had become insane, impossible. Yet she had to go through with it.

Bit by bit that old feeling of panic began to tighten in her chest. It coiled around her like a giant constrictor, attempting to squeeze the life out of her. She fought it off. She was no longer a little girl—frightened and unloved—left at home with the housekeeper while her parents disappeared for months. She was no longer a young woman facing the unrelenting pressures and cutthroat competition of the business world, struggling desperately to make a place for herself. She had grown up, become successful, confident, secure. She didn't need anyone to hold her hand, to walk by her side. She could see this through—she *would* see it through—and she'd go on with her life when it was over.

But she would still be alone.

Dana was going to kill Gabe Purvis. The minute she got him by himself, she would lock her fingers around his throat and choke the life out of him.

The instant she stepped through the church door, she knew the wedding wouldn't be anything the way he'd promised. There had to be a hundred people jammed into that little church. She hadn't known there were that many people in the whole of Iron Springs. Why couldn't it have been a weekday? They'd all still be at work.

This wasn't at all what she had envisioned for her wedding. She had planned to get married in a huge church filled with at least a thousand guests. A pipe organ and trumpets would accompany her down the long aisle. Her dress would look like a cloud of cream lace. Her train would extend for at least twenty feet and be carried by a half dozen little boys. An equal number of little girls, all dressed in pink, would strew baskets of rose petals for her to trod upon. Dozens of attendants would flank her groom who would be dressed in a formal morning coat.

Instead she entered a tiny country church, walked down an aisle barely fifty feet long, wearing a simple suit of cream silk, the only dress clothes she'd brought with her. She'd had to borrow a veil. Her corsage consisted of flowers gathered from Mrs. Purvis's yard. Danny walked down the aisle ahead of her—he looked back every few steps to make certain she was following him—carrying the wedding ring on a pillow borrowed from the preacher. Gabe, dressed in his Sunday best, waited for her down front. At least she wasn't disappointed on one score. He was as handsome as any bridegroom from her dreams.

She managed to control her emotions until they got to the vows. Up until then, she told herself she was going through the necessary steps in a game of deception to keep Danny. But when Gabe slipped the ring on her finger and said the part that began *with this ring I thee wed* she nearly lost it.

This wasn't the wedding she'd dreamed of, a bridegroom waiting at the altar who loved her desperately, who she loved more than life. This wasn't the beginning of her *happy ever after.* It wasn't the joyous occasion she longed to share with her parents and friends. It wasn't her declaration to the world that she'd achieved her dream, that now she was happy.

She told herself not to confuse this ceremony with the real thing. It was a sham, a make-believe wedding. Gabe didn't love her and she didn't love him. They were doing this to protect Danny. As soon as he was safe, the marriage would disappear like it had never been. She could still have her dream.

It didn't help that Gabe's mother cried throughout the entire ceremony. Not silently, not quietly sniffing into her handkerchief. No, every time they came to some significant line in the ceremony—*I do!* was her favorite—she'd take a shuddering breath and be off again. It was made worse by an outlandishly dressed female in purple fingernails and blue eyeshadow who sat next to Mrs. Purvis and consoled her in very audible whispers.

Dana looked forward to the recessional as an unconditional retreat.

No such luck. She'd no sooner reached the vestibule than one of the ushers told Dana they were expected in the hotel lobby immediately for a reception.

"I specifically stipulated no reception," Dana hissed in Gabe's ear.

"I had nothing to do with it. The minute the ladies heard we were getting married, they turned the town inside out putting together a reception."

"Who told them?"

"Ma. Who did you expect?"

She should have known Mrs. Purvis couldn't keep her son's marriage secret. "Why did they do it?"

"It's their way of welcoming you into the community."

She didn't believe that. It was more probably their way of scaring her half to death.

"You said they didn't like you because of your mother. This shows they don't blame you for what she did."

Why did he always have a reasonable answer for everything? Their marriage wouldn't last very long, but maybe she'd have time to teach him that a good husband knew when to abandon reason for emotion.

But he didn't know women. If she was any judge, they'd been whispering behind their veils the whole time she and Gabe were exchanging vows. They had to be wondering why the marriage was so rushed, why it had come so soon after Mattie and Mr. Purvis's deaths. Dana's cheeks felt warm just thinking of the things they must have been saying.

By the time she and Gabe had finished signing the license in the preacher's office, the church had emptied. Maybe she'd imagined the entire wedding. She coaxed Gabe into walking as slowly as possible to the hotel. She felt absolutely certain the first person she met would want to know when they were going to have their first child.

"I still don't understand why your mother's so happy," Dana said. "I thought she'd be shocked at your marrying me so fast."

"She was a little surprised," Gabe said. "Okay, she was flabbergasted, but Ma likes you. She always has. Once she got over her surprise, she started to grin. 'I always knew you had a liking for that girl,' she said. I decided it would be best if she went on thinking that.

She reminded me that Mattie always said you still liked me.''

"She didn't!" Dana exclaimed.

"Yes, she did," Gabe said. "Remember, I read all her letters, too.''

Dana felt like her old friend had stabbed her in the back. "But what about everybody else?"

"People around here pretty much accept you right off or it takes fifty years. I told you they liked you when you were a kid. They liked your grandmother, too. They really want us to be happy. Besides, they don't see it as so sudden. After all, we've known each other for more than twenty years.''

She entered the darkened hotel lobby. It would be nice to stay here. Maybe she could hide behind one of the huge ferns, let Gabe go to the reception by himself while she tried to readjust her thinking. He practically pulled her through the lobby and up the stairs to the ladies' parlor on the second floor. She stepped through the huge double doors and came to an abrupt halt.

The room was about one hundred feet long, forty feet deep, had sixteen-foot ceilings, and huge floor-to-ceiling windows on three sides. The furniture and the potted plants had been pushed against the walls and into corners. She and Gabe stood exposed to the gaze of every person present.

Every citizen of Iron Springs had squeezed into the room, mostly gathered around a table that groaned with pies, cakes, cookies, brownies and pastries, even home-made doughnuts. Since every pie and cake had already been cut, Dana knew the women had brought whatever they could find in their refrigerators. She couldn't decide whether to feel complimented or insulted.

Mrs. Purvis emerged from the crowd to give her son

a big hug. She kept on kissing him until Gabe took her by the shoulders and put her at a distance.

"Enough of that," he said smiling, a little guiltily Dana thought. "Go cry over Dana for a while."

The happy woman flung wide her arms, clasped Dana in a hug that would have done justice to a female wrestler, and pressed her to her bosom. Dana felt engulfed.

"I'm so happy," Mrs. Purvis said, weeping unashamedly, her tears falling on Dana's silk top. "I didn't think Gabe would ever get married again. I always knew he had a soft spot in his heart for you." She kissed Dana almost as many times as she kissed Gabe. "I'm so glad you forgave him. Mattie said you always liked him."

Try as she might, Dana couldn't keep her body from stiffening, but that didn't slow Mrs. Purvis's flow of chatter.

"I would have gotten a proper wedding cake from Harrisonburg if Gabe had given me more notice."

"It's all right," Dana assured her. "I wasn't expecting anything."

"We couldn't let you get married and do nothing," Hannah said. "Your poor grandmother would turn in her grave."

If her poor grandmother had any idea why she'd gotten married, she was already spinning.

The entire town lined up to congratulate Dana, shake her hand, hug and kiss her, tease her about having caught the bachelor everybody thought had made a clean getaway.

"Now the married men can put up their shotguns," Solomon Trinket said.

"I never climbed in anybody's window," Gabe said, grinning at the ancient old man.

"Who said anything about you? It's their wives they

was worried about. No man with a beer belly and a bald spot can rest easy with an unattached young colt like you about."

"I can't leave the old coot for a minute without him talking about sex," Hannah Coleman complained.

"Looking at you sure don't do it," Solomon shot back.

"It's a good thing, or I'd 'a' knocked you senseless twenty years ago."

That episode was just absurd enough to break the tension, and Dana began to relax and enjoy herself. Overwhelmed by the townspeople's goodwill, she hated to think how they'd feel when they found out what she and Gabe had done. They'd forgive him, but she'd never be welcome in Iron Springs again.

"Time to cut one of the cakes," someone called.

"Which one?"

"Let Dana choose."

Dana chose a seven-layer cake filled with jam. It looked just like the ones her grandmother used to make. For a moment she could almost imagine herself back at the farm sitting in the spotless kitchen. Life had been so sweet, so uncomplicated then. Why did everything have to be so difficult now?

"Cake," Danny announced, pushing his way forward until his nose practically touched the cake.

Dana laughed. "Give me a chance to cut it, you little pig. I'll give you a piece in a minute."

Danny didn't move until Dana handed him a slice of cake on a napkin. She broke off a piece and fed it to him. She didn't dare let him feed himself. He'd have half the cake in his mouth and the rest on the floor.

"You going to give me a piece of that cake?" Gabe asked.

"You've got to link arms first." The outlandish female with purple fingernails again. "That's *real* sexy," she cooed.

Dana felt certain she'd made that up. But when she hooked her arm with Gabe's and lifted a piece of cake to his open mouth, a feeling of suppressed excitement swept through her. She looked at his mouth and lips, *really* looked at them. She still couldn't put her finger on exactly what made them look so sexy. Maybe his mouth was a little wider, his lips a little more generous. Maybe his grin wasn't perfectly symmetrical. Maybe none of that mattered. All that really counted was that he had a mouth that made her think of kisses.

A tremor caused Dana to shudder.

"Anything wrong?" Gabe asked.

"Just a little nervous." How could she tell this man who thought she actively disliked him that she couldn't think of anything except kissing him silly, having him kiss *her* just as thoroughly?

"Open up," Gabe said.

She took only a small bite of cake. Her throat was so tight she wasn't sure she could swallow.

"Now he's supposed to lick the icing off your lips," Ms. Purple Nails said.

"I wished I'd known that at my wedding," one man said, winking at his embarrassed wife.

"There's no icing on that cake."

"He can pretend, can't he?" Ms. Purple Nails asked.

"Sure can," Gabe said.

"This wasn't in the agreement," Dana hissed, not sure she could manage this.

"It's part of the game," Gabe whispered.

Still she wasn't prepared for the shock of Gabe's tongue gently brushing her lips. Her belly tightened. She sucked in a startled breath, gripped his arm so hard she was certain her nails left imprints.

"We need more cake," Ms. Purple Nails called. "Something with lots of really sticky icing."

Dana knew she couldn't endure that. "It's time for everyone else to have some cake," she said, picking up the knife. "Who may I serve first?"

"We need bride and groom pictures," Ms. Purple Nails announced

"Who are you?" Dana finally asked. "And why are you doing this?"

"I'm Salome Halfacre, and I'm doing this because we wouldn't have any fun if I didn't. Everybody here is too stodgy."

Stodgy sounded wonderful to Dana, but apparently Salome had fractured all sense of restraint. Everyone took out cameras and demanded pictures of the happy couple.

Someone snatched the knife away, and hands pushed Dana into Gabe's arms.

"Hold her real tight," someone urged.

"Look into his eyes."

"She'll get a crick in her neck."

"Might as well let him stand tall while he can. With a body like that, she'll bring him to his knees soon enough."

Solomon Trinket again. Dana decided he must have been a real terror starting about the time of World War I. Every shotgun in the valley must have been kept oiled and ready for decades.

Dana worried that her retinas would be permanently damaged by the number of flashes that exploded in her face. Colored bubbles still burst before her eyes when an unexpected hush fell on the room. Her eyes finally came into focus, and she found herself facing a rotund little man.

"Are you Gabriel Purvis?" he demanded of Gabe.

"Who are you?" Salome demanded. "And what are you doing at a private party?"

Dana had to give the man credit. The startling sight of Salome's purple fingernails, blue eyeshadow and lipstick that could only be described as vampire crimson, held him mesmerized for only a moment.

"I'm looking for Gabriel Purvis."

"You found him," Gabe said. "Who are you?"

"Who's that?" the man asked, indicating Dana.

"Can't you recognize a bride when you see one?" Salome asked.

That piece of news didn't sit well with the man. "Are you the one who got married?"

"I don't see that's any concern of yours," Gabe said.

"I'm Chester Dowd," he announced, "attorney for Lucius Abernathy, Danny Abernathy's natural father."

Dana felt herself go rigid. She'd forgotten all about Lucius and his lawyer.

"His name's Danny Purvis," Gabe said.

"Not for long," the lawyer said. "I'm here to let you know I filed a request last week for custody on behalf of my client."

"If you filed it in New York, it has no validity in Virginia," Dana said.

He spun on her angrily. "You got out of New York very fast, didn't you?"

Dana didn't trust herself to answer.

"What my wife did or didn't do is not the issue here," Gabe said.

"Wife!" he exclaimed, clearly shocked despite the evidence of a wedding he must already have noted.

"Duh!" Salome said. "That's why they're hugging and kissing and having their picture taken. I thought you had to be intelligent to be a lawyer."

"This is a fake," the lawyer said.

"I can assure you it's not," the Reverend Pike said. "I performed the ceremony. They have signed the proper licenses."

"It's a put-up job so they can steal my client's son."

Chapter Eight

Dana's heart leaped into her throat. What would the people who'd been celebrating their wedding think? She'd played a trick on them, and this man had exposed it right before their eyes.

"I can assure you the marriage is genuine," Reverend Pike repeated.

"Nonsense," Mr. Dowd said. "I have a complete file on Miss Marsh. I know every man she's dated for the past ten years. This man isn't one of them."

"My son and his wife have known each other since they were children," Mrs. Purvis said.

"He used to serve her ice cream cones in my store," Hannah said. "Gave her twice as much ice cream as he ought."

Some of the townspeople laughed.

"Used to talk about her all the time," one man said. "I thought they shoulda got married years ago."

"That's neither here nor there," Mr. Dowd said, trying to regain the floor.

But no one would let him. First one person than another insisted upon recounting an incident that convinced them Dana and Gabe had been in love for years, that only a cruel accident of fate—in the form of Ellen—had prevented them from marrying sooner.

Dana could hardly believe her ears. No one believed Mr. Dowd. What's more, they were doing their best to convince him they had known from the first how things would turn out.

"We've talked enough," Salome declared. "Kiss her," she ordered Gabe. "Show this Yankee coon dog that mountain folk don't lie when it comes to love."

"My pleasure," Gabe said, flashing a brilliant smile at the lawyer. "And you don't have to worry about getting a good picture the first time," he said. "We'll do this as often as necessary."

Chuckles greeted his sally. Solomon Trinket's earthy comment caused Dana to blush.

"For God's sake, look as if you're enjoying this," Gabe hissed before he took her in his arms and gave her a kiss that took her breath away.

Instead of enjoyment, Dana felt stunned, shocked, mesmerized, petrified—virtually any emotion that indicated uncontrolled fear and bone-deep panic. Under the triple assault of fear for Danny, alarm over the prospect of Gabe's kiss and embarrassment at being forced to perform before the whole town, she felt the usual panic when things went out of control. That made her reaction to Gabe's kiss even more frightening.

Being in his arms, being held tight against his body, swept away all the constraints that enabled her to control her feelings. The kiss swept away all the lies she'd been telling herself for the past fourteen years. She hadn't ceased to think of Gabe or to compare every man she met to him. With just a little encouragement—maybe as little as another kiss or two—she could become infatuated all over again. Her whole structure of self-deception came tumbling down with a resounding crash.

She emerged from the kiss breathless, flushed, terrified.

"Kiss her again," someone called. "My flash didn't work."

"I couldn't get a good shot with so many people in the way."

Gabe took her in his arms, bent her so low she thought for a moment he was going to lay her on the floor, then kissed her with all the flair of a Hollywood Latin lover.

"Again."

"No."

But Dana's protest got lost in the chorus of requests for just one more picture. Events seemed to swirl around her, disconnected, random, unreal, until the preacher's voice broke through the clamor.

"We've required this poor couple to perform like circus animals long enough," he said, his deep displeasure directed at Mr. Dowd. "They have to visit with their guests before heading off on their honeymoon. If you've got anything else to say, I suggest you say it to his lawyer. Marshall, take this man over to your house and give him a stiff whisky."

Mr. Dowd didn't want to leave, but several husky men propelled him from the room.

"We haven't had time to plan a honeymoon," Gabe said.

"I don't think it's a good idea to leave Danny just yet," Dana added.

"You should go somewhere," the minister said. "Why not take her to Harrisonburg to dinner?"

"Then you could find a motel and stay overnight," Salome added.

"Young people in my day didn't need no motels," Solomon Trinket said. "A man had enough sass about him to take his woman anywhere they be."

Dana couldn't believe she was standing in the midst of a sea of virtual strangers discussing arrangements for her honeymoon. She didn't want to go to Harrisonburg for dinner or anything else. She wanted to get back to the house, make certain Danny was okay, then lock herself in the bedroom.

They didn't pose for any more pictures, but Gabe kept his arm around her. She supposed that was the smart thing to do, but it took every bit of control she had left to keep from moving away from him. Their bodies made constant contact, her breast against his chest, her hip against his hip, his arm across her back and around her waist. Every time Gabe moved the slightest bit—and he seemed to be in constant motion—their bodies rubbed together. It caused Dana to forget the ends of her sentences, to lose threads of conversation.

Whenever this happened, Salome would wink at her and grin. The sight of that blue eyelid moving up and down, like a beach house awning in a hurricane, intensified the unreality of the past hour.

Finally, when she'd begun to think the reception would never end, the ladies started gathering up their cakes, pies and melting ice cream.

"You don't have to hurry back," Salome said. "I can sleep over with Danny."

"Danny stays with me," Mrs. Purvis said.

"We can both stay," Salome said, giving Gabe a

broad leer. "It's the only way I'm going to get into Gabe's bed."

Everyone laughed, no one harder than Salome. She pinched Gabe's arm but turned to Dana.

"You got a good one in his prime," she said. "Don't waste him. Most men around here go to seed real fast. Except my great-granddad. He's just as randy as he was seventy years ago."

Dana wondered how she'd missed knowing Salome during the summers she visited her grandmother. She must have been a small child. But it was hard to imagine anyone like this woman had ever been a child. Despite her outlandish makeup, Dana felt drawn to this candid, brash, even rude, young woman. She just might be irreverent enough to befriend an outsider.

"You better treat him real good," Salome whispered in her ear. "After what his first wife did to him, we thought he'd never get married again."

Involuntarily Dana turned to look at Gabe. What could Salome mean by that?

"I never thought to see you back in the shop today," Sam said when Gabe arrived shortly after two o'clock.

"We're still behind on orders," Gabe said.

He hadn't returned to the shop because orders had piled up or because he hadn't worked more than a few hours since Dana had pulled into town yesterday.

Yesterday. It seemed impossible so much could have happened in such a short time. Yet in less than twenty-four hours, he'd let this woman turn his life upside down.

No. Circumstances stemming from Mattie's death had caused the disruption of his life. Dana just happened to be caught up in the mess with him. If it had been anybody but Dana, he could have shrugged it off, done what he had to do and moved on.

He would still move on—he didn't have any choice—but things would never be quite the same. At least, he wouldn't be. He had let himself become infatuated with a woman he'd once hurt badly. And he'd become that way despite the fact she didn't want such a complication any more than he did.

"It's your wedding day. You ought to be celebrating with your wife," Sam said.

"We're going to Harrisonburg this evening."

"You should be with her now."

"And watch her feed Danny then watch him take a nap?"

"There's other things you could be doing instead of watching that kid sleep." Sam winked and gave him a broad grin.

That's exactly the reason Gabe had returned to the shop. He couldn't get his mind off those *other things*. He didn't understand that. He hadn't thought about her in years.

But as he moved to the sideboard he'd been sanding in preparation for the first coat of shellac, he realized that wasn't true. Every letter from Mattie contained news of Dana. She appeared in more than half the pictures. He couldn't help but notice that she'd become even more attractive with maturity. He used to think that had no more effect on him than looking at pictures of some supermodel or movie star.

But seeing Dana in the flesh had changed all of that. Being married to her could turn into a razor-sharp, two-edged sword.

"There'll be time for that tonight," Billy told Sam.

"I'll bet you five dollars we have to open up tomorrow."

"Hell, I've got better ways to lose my money than that," Sam said, grinning and winking back.

Both men broke up over their own jokes, but Gabe didn't laugh. Thoughts of Dana's body had been driving him crazy from the moment during the reception he'd taken her in his arms and kissed her. The feel of her body against his, her sweet mouth and soft lips, had destroyed the barrier he'd built in his mind against her attractiveness.

Then that damned lawyer had arrived.

His presence irritated Gabe, but it was the kisses, the standing for what seemed like hours with his arm around Dana, their bodies pressed close together, that had been his undoing. He could kill Salome and Reverend Pike for insisting they have a honeymoon.

The mere sound of the word had nearly knocked the pins out from under him. It was inhuman to hold out to a man something Mother Nature had ordained he should want and need, while decency and morality decreed even more firmly he couldn't have it. Gabe felt like a muddy field after a hard-fought football game, chewed up and hardly recognizable.

But what bothered him the most—well maybe not the most, but it bothered him a lot—was the fact he could be so desperate to make love to a woman he'd told himself for years he didn't like or respect.

It wouldn't be making love. It would be sex, plain and simple. And while he wasn't opposed to that now and then, that wasn't an option with Dana. If he ever once let down the barriers, he'd never again get the situation between him and Dana back the way it ought to be. The way it *had* to be.

* * *

"Thank you for dinner," Dana said to Gabe as they neared Iron Springs. "I didn't know you could find such good food in Harrisonburg."

"A few people in the wilderness do know how to cook."

They'd both been snapping at each other, taking everything the wrong way. "I didn't mean it like that."

"Actually, I think the cook moved here from Massachusetts. So I guess we can't claim credit for him. One more point for New England."

"Why are you doing this?"

"What?"

"Taking everything I say the wrong way."

"I don't know how to take the things you say. I don't know you. I only know you wouldn't have come back to Iron Springs without being forced, that you don't think much of us."

"That's not true."

"Then you admire us. Good, I guess, but I hope you won't try to convince your friends to move to Iron Springs. The place won't be the same."

"At least it would wake up. I think it's been asleep longer than Brigadoon."

Now she'd done it. She'd disparaged his town. That was only a hair's breadth less terrible than making rude comments about his relatives. "Look, I didn't mean that, but you've been jumping on me all evening. If you thought you were going to hate being married to me so much, why did you do it?"

"To keep Danny."

She knew that. He didn't have to keep saying it from between gritted teeth

"I don't hate being married to you," he said.

"You sure had me fooled."

"I'm nervous about being married."

"Why? We've agreed on everything. I won't go back on my promises."

"It's not that."

"Then what is it?" She couldn't picture Gabe being nervous. Even harder to think anything she had done could have caused it.

"Maybe it's having my routine upset. Having you and Danny in my house doesn't really bother me, but I'm not used to it."

He wasn't telling the truth. She had been the one to flounder about, rudderless and incapable of organizing her thoughts or controlling her feelings. He had known what he intended to do from the first.

"It could be the lawyer," she suggested. "I know Marshall warned us he was coming, but his showing up at the reception shocked me."

"It's a shame you can't jail a man for doing something like that."

At last they were in agreement on something. But as the car rolled across the tiny bridge and entered Iron Springs, she felt the tension between them escalate further.

The entire evening had been tense. There had been times when she wondered how she'd managed to swallow food. When they got in the car to drive home, it became even worse. She wanted to get as far away from him as possible, but she forced herself to sit exactly in the middle of her seat.

But even that had been too close. She didn't need to touch Gabe to be acutely aware of his presence. Energy flowed from his body like light from fire. She'd dated a couple of men like that, but never one with the power to attract that Gabe possessed.

"I wonder how your mother and Danny got along," she said. When they left for Harrisonburg, she'd thought she'd be worried about Danny all night. Though she had thought of him frequently, her concern lacked the urgency she'd expected. Elton had agreed to come over. Danny showed signs of hero worship when it came to Elton.

"I'm sure they got along fine," Gabe said. "Ma has a knack for dealing with children. She loves them, and they love her right back."

Love had a way of overturning barriers. It was hard to distrust someone you loved or who loved you. You just naturally sensed you'd be safe with them. Odd she should feel perfectly safe with Gabe in one sense, practically terrified of him in another.

No, it's yourself you're afraid of.

That didn't help. She trusted Gabe to keep his word. She didn't know about herself.

They pulled into the driveway. She got out of the car ahead of Gabe.

"We ought to go in together," he said. "The way you sprinted for the door, somebody might think we'd just had a fight."

"I'm worried about Danny."

She made herself wait. It felt funny, his opening the door for her, allowing her to enter first, coming into a hall that practically had his name stenciled on the walls. She could almost feel the house sending her an unspoken message. *Alien territory. Keep out!*

Mrs. Purvis came out into the hall from the den before they reached the door. The sight of her smiling, cheerful face banished some of the tension that had permeated

the evening. No world filled with people as uncomplicated and straightforward as Gabe's mother could be entirely out of balance.

"Did you have a nice time?" she asked.

"How's Danny?" Dana asked. "Where is he?"

"He's asleep."

"When did he go to bed?" It hurt a little to know
he'd gone to sleep without her reading to him. Another
piece of the fabric of her life shredded. By the time Gabe
divorced her, there wouldn't be anything left.

"I put him down at seven-thirty just after Elton left.
He fretted a little at first. He missed you, but I read to
him until he went to sleep."

She ought not be grateful that missing her made
Danny unhappy, but she was selfish enough to feel better
that he did. "I'll just go check on him."

"I'll see Ma home," Gabe said.

She nodded and climbed the stairs to Danny's room.
It gave her an odd feeling to enter the unfamiliar room.
She had known every inch of Danny's old room, could
put her hand on anything she wanted even in the dark.
Light from the street lamp—one of the few signs Iron
Springs had entered the twentieth century—illuminated
all but the darkened corners of his room.

Danny slept on his side, his teddy bear clutched
lightly to his chest. He had his thumb in his mouth. He
always did that when he was upset. Being very gentle
so she wouldn't wake him, Dana pulled it out of his
mouth. The released pressure caused a tiny pop. Danny
stirred restlessly. He hugged his teddy tighter, pulled his
knees up higher.

She leaned over and kissed him on the cheek. His skin
felt so soft and warm. He looked heartbreakingly an-
gelic.

"He looks real peaceful."

Dana started, took a noisy breath. She turned to find Gabe at her side. "You scared me half to death," she whispered. "I didn't hear you come up."

"I didn't want to wake Danny."

She still couldn't imagine why she hadn't heard him. Though he didn't carry any fat on his tall, well-muscled body, he had to weigh more than two hundred pounds. She couldn't believe that not a single board in the wood floors squeaked.

"How did you get back so fast?"

"I never left. Ma took my car." He looked down at Danny. "He looks so little and helpless."

"He *is* little and helpless."

"It didn't feel that way when he wanted the train."

"Never come between a child and his toys. Especially after they become men." Now she was making the unnecessary needling remarks. "We'd better go before we wake him."

They tiptoed back into the hall. Gabe's shoes made no noise. Hers did.

"I want to leave the door open in case he wakes up," she said.

"You'd better close it until we're ready for bed. Sounds travel in this old house."

All the tension of the evening came hurtling back with a vengeance. The notion of getting undressed and slipping into bed collided with the realization Gabe would be doing the same thing in an adjacent room. The resulting explosion sent her temperature through the roof.

"I have only one bathroom upstairs," Gabe said. "You'd better go first."

Chapter Nine

Dana didn't move.

"I can go first," Gabe said.

"That's probably better," she said. "I'll probably take longer."

"I shower and shave at night."

"You go first, anyway."

A little while later she wasn't sure she'd made the right decision. The sound of water running in the shower brought images of Gabe's naked body to mind. Before the water stopped running, she'd turned him into a cross between Michelangelo's David and one of the chariot drivers in Neptune's Fountain at the Palace of Versailles. The image of bulging muscles, powerful torso and classic beauty—all stripped of inhibiting clothing—made her so hot she couldn't sit still.

But she could do nothing but wait for him to finish. She'd gone through her night bag twice, rearranged everything, trying to keep her mind off Gabe, but she couldn't banish the image of him standing before the sink, still unclothed, shaving. The play of muscles across his back, the slimming of his torso to his waist, the swell of his bottom, the contour of his powerful thighs—

She got up with a muttered curse. She had to think of something else, or she would melt into a puddle right there.

Or jump Gabe when he came out of the bathroom.

The thought startled her so, she sat back down. Had she forgotten the past so thoroughly she could actually contemplate getting into bed with him—worse, *want* to go to bed with him?

Yes...and no.

That answer didn't help. Her body lusted after him, but her mind said he was incapable of seeing past her outer shell. Somewhere in the space in between, her emotions wandered lost and confused, desperately trying to bring about a compromise. If she could have foreseen the events of the past thirty-six hours, she'd have escaped with Danny to her mother in Switzerland and dared Gabe or Lucius to find her.

She almost laughed aloud. It mortified her mother to admit she had a thirty-year-old daughter, especially an unmarried one. But she would have had an apoplectic fit if Dana had showed up with Danny.

"Your turn. I left the window open to clear out some of the steam."

Dana started violently.

"Are you all right?"

"You startled me."

"You acted like you were scared to death."

"I was just thinking."

He looked doubtful, but she didn't intend to explain. She felt at a major disadvantage already.

"I've got space laid out for a bathroom between this room and the next," he said. "But with just me living here, I didn't see going to the bother of putting it in."

"That's no problem. It's not as though I'm in a hurry to go anywhere."

She just wanted him to leave. He probably considered himself modestly dressed. But a bathrobe open at the throat and barely reaching his knees wasn't nearly enough for her. She thought the Islamic rule of covering their women from head to foot ought to be applied to men like Gabe.

"Are you sure you have everything you need?" he asked.

"Yes."

"Do you know where everything is. I can show you if—"

"It's a bathroom, Gabe. We have them in New York. I'll figure it out."

A strained smiled lightened his expression. "If there's nothing else, I'm going to bed. I get up at six-thirty. Want me to wake you?"

No. She wanted him out of the house before she woke. "I suppose you'd better. There must be things we need to talk about."

"What?"

"I don't know. I'm too tired to think. Just wake me up."

He lingered. She didn't move. She didn't want to have to walk past him, to come so near she could touch him. She might do it.

"If there's nothing else…"

"I can't think of anything," she said.

"Well, good night."

"Good night."

"Thanks for agreeing to marry me."

"As you said, it's for Danny's sake."

"Yeah."

She didn't know why he seemed disappointed. That's what he'd been telling her all evening.

"I hope the bed's comfortable."

"It was last night. I suppose it will be tonight, too."

He grinned. "I'd better go to bed. We're beginning to sound as if we haven't a brain between us."

"Would you lock the doors?" she asked.

"We don't need to."

"I know, but I can't sleep if you don't."

"Okay. But before you leave, you're going to learn to sleep like a baby with both doors standing wide open."

She would never be able to sleep like a baby in this house. But it had nothing to do with unlocked doors. The danger was inside.

Gabe looked at the clock. Six o'clock. He wondered if he'd had as much as six minutes of sound sleep. He'd spent most of the night tossing restlessly in his bed, acutely aware Dana slept only a few feet away.

It might as well have been a thousand miles. They were separated by more than the wall. It seemed unnecessarily perverse of his physical nature—or whatever part of him he could blame it on—to keep torturing him with images of what could be if...

There could be no *if*. Despite trying to give the appearance of a happily married couple, she wanted him to stay as far away from her as possible. That shouldn't

have been so hard. They were already separated in every
other way.

He had been okay until the wedding. But the reception, more specifically, the hugging and kissing they'd
done to convince Mr. Dowd, had been his undoing. By
the time they left the hotel, his nerves were wound so
tight, he could hardly stand it. If Dana had indicated
even the slightest willingness, he'd have taken her
straight to his bedroom and made love to her the entire
afternoon.

Okay, it would have been sex. But it would have been
sex like he'd never experienced with any another
woman.

He could still taste her kisses, had been tasting them
during dinner, during the drive back from Harrisonburg,
during the long hours he'd lain awake remembering,
imagining, being tortured by what he knew he couldn't
have, shouldn't want. She'd been reluctant to kiss him,
but once her body betrayed her, she seemed to enjoy it
as much as he did. Knowing that had provided fuel for
his imagination.

Neither of them had anticipated the heat that flared
between them as they stood together, their bodies
pressed against each other, smiling stupidly for dozens
of flash cameras. After more than a dozen relatively
peaceful bachelor years, he couldn't understand how one
woman could unhinge him so. No other woman had, and
quite a few had tried.

He had been a rotten dinner companion. His uncontrolled response to her angered him, and he'd taken it
out on her. He hadn't acted that way with other women,
so it *had* to be Dana's fault. Not even a cold shower had
alleviated his uncomfortable condition.

Now he'd lain awake most of the night, imagining

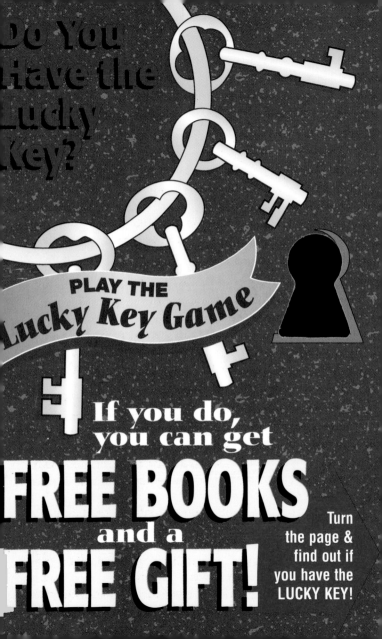

PLAY THE
Lucky Key Game
and get

HOW TO PLAY:

1. With a coin, carefully scratch off gold area at the right. Then check the claim chart to see what we have for you —**FREE BOOKS** and a **FREE GIFT** — **ALL YOURS FREE!**

2. Send back this card and you'll receive brand-new Silhouette Special Edition® novels. These books have a cover price of $4.25 each in the U.S. and $4.75 each in Canada, but they are yours to keep absolutely free.

3. There's no catch. You're under no obligation to buy anything. We charge nothing — ZERO — for your first shipment. And you don't have to make any minimum number of purchases — not even one!

4. The fact is thousands of readers enjoy receiving books by mail from the Silhouette Reader Service™ months before they're available in stores. They like the convenience of home delivery and they love our discount prices!

5. We hope that after receiving your free books you'll want to remain a subscriber. But the choice is yours — to continue or cancel, any time at all! So why not take us up on our invitation, with no risk of any kind. You'll be glad you did!

YOURS FREE!
A SURPRISE MYSTERY GIFT

We can't tell you what it is...but we're sure you'll like it! A
FREE GIFT—
just for playing the LUCKY KEY game!

FREE GIFTS!

NO COST! NO OBLIGATION TO BUY!
NO PURCHASE NECESSARY!

The Silhouette Reader Service™ — Here's how it works:

Accepting your 2 free books and gift places you under no obligation to buy anything. You may keep the books and gift and return the shipping statement marked "cancel." If you do not cancel, about a month later we'll send you 6 additional novels and bill you just $3.57 each in the U.S., or $3.96 each in Canada, plus 25¢ delivery per book and applicable taxes if any.* That's the complete price and — compared to cover prices of $4.25 each in the U.S. and $4.75 each in Canada — it's quite a bargain! You may cancel at any time, but if you choose to continue, every month we'll send you 6 more books, which you may either purchase at the discount price or return to us and cancel your subscription.

*Terms and prices subject to change without notice. Sales tax applicable in N.Y. Canadian residents will be charged applicable provincial taxes and GST.

If offer card is missing write to: Silhouette Reader Service, 3010 Walden Ave., P.O. Box 1867, Buffalo, NY 14240-1867

BUSINESS REPLY MAIL
FIRST-CLASS MAIL   PERMIT NO. 717   BUFFALO, NY

POSTAGE WILL BE PAID BY ADDRESSEE

SILHOUETTE READER SERVICE
3010 WALDEN AVE
PO BOX 1867
BUFFALO NY 14240-9952

NO POSTAGE
NECESSARY
IF MAILED
IN THE
UNITED STATES

scenes that would never happen, hearing words they'd never say, thinking of outcomes that were impossible. He needed to go to work, become involved with a new project, hit his thumb with a hammer—anything to get his mind off Dana.

Mumbling a curse, he threw the covers aside. It didn't take long to get dressed. He went downstairs in his stocking feet so he wouldn't wake Dana. He'd fix his coffee and get out of the house before she woke. Maybe returning to his normal routine would help.

He didn't get a chance to test his theory. He'd just put the water on to boil when Dana entered the kitchen with a very wide-awake Danny on her hip.

The shock of seeing her in his kitchen at this hour of the morning, wearing nothing but a silk bathrobe that didn't cover much of her gorgeous legs, and a dreamy, half-asleep expression on her face, affected him like a punch in the stomach. She looked so much like the sweet little girl he remembered he could almost think she was the same person. He'd been trained his entire life to protect women, to be constantly on guard for their welfare. At this moment Dana looked exactly like the kind of woman he would want to protect, to safeguard, to cherish.

He told himself to stop imagining things. Dana might look charmingly helpless right now, but it was an illusion. This woman could hold her own in New York. She could probably flatten Iron Springs and everybody in it if she had a mind to.

"I didn't mean to wake you," he said.

"You didn't," she said, smothering a yawn. "Danny did. He usually sleeps longer, but I guess the break in routine has thrown him off schedule."

"Want me to fix him some breakfast?"

"I've got his cereal."

"Want eggs," Danny announced.

"I've got your favorite cereal," Dana said. "It'll be ready in a minute."

"Want eggs," Danny repeated.

Dana didn't appear to be pleased with his choice, but she didn't argue. "Apparently he prefers eggs to cereal," she said to Gabe.

"It's no trouble. How about you?"

"All right, and some bacon, too."

"Sure your metabolism won't go into shock?"

She laughed. "Grandmother used to feed me eggs and sausage every morning. I guess my metabolism can survive for another day."

"I'll do the eggs and bacon if you'll do the rest. There's butter and jam in the refrigerator and—"

"Don't tell me. I might as well get used to finding things by myself. You won't want to cook breakfast for us every morning."

The idea appealed to him, even though he hadn't eaten breakfast in years. "It's no more trouble to cook for three than for one."

"I'll clean up."

He liked that. He hated doing dishes. Even with a dishwasher, they sometimes piled up in the sink.

"I don't like Danny sitting on that stack of phone books," Dana said. "He could fall."

"No problem. I'll make him a high chair." He'd never made one, but he looked forward to it.

By the time Dana got the table set and he served the food, he'd spent more time than he did on an entire meal when by himself. But the time had passed quickly and pleasantly. He enjoyed having someone in the kitchen with him. Danny's chatter served to brighten his morning rather than irritate him.

"Is he always this cheerful in the morning?" he asked.

"Always. Sometimes Mattie and I would draw straws to see who'd get up with him."

That didn't sound like his sister. "I'm surprised Mattie could sleep through somebody else taking care of her child."

Dana chuckled. "Neither of us could. We'd both end up in the kitchen, our eyelids propped open, mumbling incoherently to each other."

He'd like to have seen that. The thought of waking up and finding her sleeping next to him caused the fire to ignite in his loins. He served the last of the eggs and sat down before his condition could become obvious.

Dana was annoyed when Gabe fed Danny from his own plate.

"I can feed him," she said.

"I figured as much. But since I'm going to be doing it alone in a few weeks, I might as well get some practice."

The reminder that she would soon have to leave Danny probably accounted for the abrupt dip in her mood, but the phrase would pop up in their conversation many times during the next weeks. It would be easier if she got used to it now.

Still, he felt sorry for her. When she first arrived, he'd thought of her as Danny's custodian. Since then he'd had plenty of opportunity to see that Dana loved Danny almost as much as she would have loved her own child. It wouldn't be easy to leave him. Gabe would do what he could to make the separation easier—encourage her to call, let her visit as often as she wanted—but separation was inevitable. He couldn't imagine her forsaking New York to be near Danny, not even for the summer.

"I've decided to put Danny in day care."

Dana's announcement caught him completely off guard. It also made him angry. *He* would soon be in sole charge of Danny, not Dana. He should be the one to make that decision.

"Why would you do that?" he asked, trying to keep his tone conversational.

"I suppose I should have discussed it with you," she said, looking slightly abashed.

That was as close to an apology as he imagined Dana would come. "We're about to discuss it," he said. "Now tell me why you think this is a good idea."

Dana flashed a brief smile. "Very diplomatically put. I think *we* ought to do it for two reasons. First, Danny needs to learn to play with other children, to relate to people his own age. There's no such thing as privacy or keeping to yourself in this town. That will take some getting used to."

"Is that why you never came back, too many people sticking their noses into your business?"

"We're not discussing me."

He shouldn't have asked that question, but he'd always wondered. He thought she liked Iron Springs, that it gave her the feeling of family and belonging her own parents were too busy to provide. He must have been wrong. She hadn't set foot in the place in fourteen years.

"What's your second reason?"

"Danny want down."

She looked at Gabe, a question in her eyes.

"Let him get down. He can't hurt anything."

"It's clear you know nothing about children," Dana said. "They've been known to destroy reinforced concrete. You can get down," Dana said to Danny, "but don't touch anything. If you see something you want, come ask me."

"You can play with anything you want in your room," Gabe said.

But Danny wasn't ready to venture that far from Dana. He went out into the hall, disappeared into the den, but he kept coming out into the hall to make sure Dana was still close by.

"My second reason," Dana continued, "is he needs to get used to whoever will take care of him when I leave...go back to New York. You and your mother both work."

"Mother is thinking of cutting back."

"He seems to be getting along famously with Elton," Dana said, "but he'll be back in school soon. Danny needs to learn to get along on his own."

"You could put it off until fall."

"I want to make sure he's settled and happy before I leave. The sooner we start, the sooner I'll find out if there're going to be any problems."

"Naomi says the other kids like him."

"I still think we ought to start now."

She hadn't eaten a bite since she started talking about leaving, just pushed her eggs about the plate, cut her bacon into smaller and smaller bits until it looked as though it had been through a meat grinder. He wished he could have sent her back to New York yesterday. The more he understood the hurt this separation would cause, the worse he felt about it.

"You realize that no matter what explanation you make, this will start speculation."

"I know."

"You won't like some of the things people will say."

"I know that, too. That's why I want you to go with me. They might think I'm putting him in day care to get rid of him. They wouldn't believe that of you."

"Oh, yes, they would."

"Well they won't believe it for long, not after they see the way you spoil him. You really have to watch that. He looks so innocent you want to give him anything he wants, but you can't. He can wrap you around his little finger in no time."

Gabe laughed. "How did you escape his snare?"

"Mattie said he'd have it rough when he grew up. No matter how modern we Americans think we are, people still don't let a child forget his birth. She didn't want Danny to grow up expecting things to come easily."

"Then Danny is in the right place. People here won't let him get too big for his britches, but they'll all be in his corner if he ever needs them."

"That's about the only reason I can stand to leave him."

Gabe heard the catch in her voice, saw moisture glisten in her eyes.

"I'd better make myself decent to be seen in public." Dana got up from the table quickly, turned away so he couldn't see her tears. "Leave the dishes. I'll clean up when I get back."

Gabe got up and took his plate to the sink. No matter what he said to himself, he couldn't help feeling guilty for causing Dana so much unhappiness. He racked his brain for a way around it, or to make it easier. He was so deep in thought he didn't realize he'd cleaned up the whole kitchen until Dana came back downstairs.

"Want down," Danny said.

"All right, little fella," Gabe said. He stood to lift

Danny from the high chair he'd made that day. "I put a box of toys in the den. Now you don't have to go all the way upstairs."

"I was going to ask if you minded if I brought some of his things downstairs," Dana said.

She'd been surprised when Gabe came home with the high chair. He said it hadn't taken much time to make, but it looked too ornate to have been made in a couple of hours. Besides, the time had been taken from his usual work. From what Mattie had said, nothing ever kept Gabe from his work. Dana considered the high chair a good sign Gabe wouldn't get so wrapped up in his work he'd neglect Danny.

"You can put his toys anywhere you want," Gabe said. "I put them in his room because it seemed the most logical place."

"It was, but he likes to be near us."

"You mean he likes to be near you. He checks on you every few minutes."

Gabe couldn't hide his disappointment that Danny hadn't accepted him as an equal part of his world.

"What do you suggest I do to change that?" Gabe asked.

"Be around him as much as possible, do things with him. He needs to get used to you, to know you're safe."

"You can't mean he thinks I'd hurt him!"

"No, but you're really big. Maybe a little frightening. He needs to learn not to be afraid of your size."

"He won't learn that always going to you."

"I can't push him away. That wouldn't work either."

She hoped they weren't about to argue. The entire day had been comfortable, reassuring. She would hate to have it end on a sour note.

They'd fixed dinner together. He'd grilled pork chops

and fixed mashed potatoes. She'd fixed a salad, steamed some beans, and unmolded the gelatin dessert she'd fixed that afternoon. She had little experience in the kitchen and certainly couldn't cook as well as he could, but she didn't want him thinking she had spent her life eating in restaurants. She didn't want him taking Danny to fast-food joints. If he had to live at the end of the earth, he ought to have decent, home-cooked meals as compensation.

"You have to do things with him," Dana explained. "Feeding him is a good place to start. So is putting him in and out of his high chair, playing with the train. It may not seem like much, but it's important."

Dinner had passed off well. Gabe had asked about her day, she asked about his, and both acted as though they were interested in the answers. She would have liked to know more about what he did.

But they talked mostly about Danny. And listened to him talk about day care. Dana gave Gabe high marks for enduring the child's endless chatter. Adults who weren't used to children generally didn't have much tolerance for them, but Gabe displayed no impatience with Danny. He seemed perfectly willing to concentrate his entire attention on Danny and ignore her completely.

Gabe got up from the table and carried his dishes to the sink. "We'd better start cleaning up."

She'd looked forward to talking to him a little more. She'd spent the morning by herself and the afternoon with Danny. As much as she loved the child, she was starved for adult company.

"You scrape, and I'll put then in the dishwasher," Gabe said.

No matter how quickly she did her part of the job, his

hand was always out, ready for the next pot or plate or glass.

"We've got all night," she said when his impatience began to grate on her nerves.

"No, we don't. I have exactly one hour before Danny goes to bed to play with him so he can get used to me."

She wondered if he would manage to save a few minutes for her. She knew this marriage was nothing more than a business arrangement, but since he was the only person she knew, she had to talk to him or watch one of the three TV channels they could get in the valley. Gabe said he never watched TV, so he didn't have a satellite dish.

"Done," Gabe said as he closed the dishwasher and put it on.

"Would you like some coffee?" Dana asked, just about the time he disappeared through the doorway.

"Sure," came his voice floating out from the den.

She took coffee beans from the freezer and measured three tablespoons into the grinder. The rasping sound of the blades as they ground the beans into tiny pieces exactly suited her mood. She'd make Gabe's coffee and take it to him. But he would pay her some attention. She refused to be upstaged by a two-year-old, even one as precious as Danny.

But as she waited for the water to boil, the noises from the den suddenly changed in volume and intensity. By the time the coffee was ready, it sounded as if World War III were taking place on the other side of the kitchen wall.

When she reached the den, she found Gabe and Danny in the middle of a fierce battle. Danny's soldiers attacked Gabe's soldiers to the accompaniment of loud explosions and impacts of crashing plastic. She'd never imagined a man could make so many realistic noises with his mouth, nor that Gabe would be the one doing it. Danny's efforts to imitate him sounded like tiny soprano squeaks to Gabe's rumbling baritone.

Why did men always have to play games of violence? She supposed that question would be asked only by a woman who'd been brought up by a succession of women and educated by women. Not that she expected Gabe and Danny to play with dolls, but Danny had blocks, puzzles, picture books and dozens of animals. If he really needed to work off some energy, he could have gotten out the peg board and hammer Mattie bought him just before she died.

But no, he preferred to engage in combat with action figures dressed in nerve-jarring blue and green and armed with lances, hatchets and guns of every type. She assumed the figures lying abandoned on their faces were the ones that had already perished in this brief-but-deadly war. With bright eyes and intent expression, Danny vigorously attacked Gabe's forces.

Dana settled on the sofa. Neither male gave any sign of being aware of her presence. The combat raged unabated while she sipped her coffee. She felt left out, ignored, and she didn't like it.

"Your coffee's getting cold," she told Gabe.

"I'll get it in a moment," he said without looking up.

He could have thanked her for bringing it, but he probably took it for granted. After all, didn't all women make coffee? Now she was being unfair. He'd fixed his own coffee for years.

She was being unfair because she felt excluded. The men obviously weren't going to sit on the sofa. She actually considered getting down in the floor with them but changed her mind. This was Gabe's time, his chance to build a rapport with Danny. They would soon have do without her all the time.

That thought made her even more depressed.

The battle escalated as Danny and Gabe brought up the reserves. With a battle figure in each hand, they couldn't manipulate the swords and other weapons. They just banged their warriors into each other. Dana thought it a crazy game. They loved it.

She considered asking them to play something more civilized, but changed her mind. And as much as she didn't understand it, this raging war seemed to be doing more to bring them together than anything Gabe had done so far.

Gabe used his man to pin Danny's man to the floor. The little boy tried everything he could, but he wasn't strong enough to push Gabe away. Dana started to speak up. She didn't think Gabe should use his obviously greater strength like that.

Just then Danny abandoned his defeated warrior, got to his feet and launched himself at Gabe. The two of them went over in a heap, Danny virtually disappearing in a tangle of Gabe's arms and legs.

Instinct caused Dana to rise half out of her chair, to want to pull Danny back to safety, to tell Gabe to be careful, to stop wrestling. A man his size could seriously hurt a child as small as Danny.

Danny's laughter caused her to pause. He wasn't fighting Gabe, he was trying to tickle him. Gabe tickled him back, and Danny shrieked with happiness. They rolled around on the floor like two puppies. At first Dana sat on the edge of her chair, worried Gabe might accidentally hurt Danny. But after a moment she relaxed. Gabe exercised great care, and Danny appeared happier than he'd been since his mother died. She guessed this

was an example of that mysterious male bonding Mattie
said Danny needed. Dana just wished Mattie had thought
to explain how it worked. She didn't have any brothers.
She'd never have guessed their rituals could be so crazy.

She settled back to wait until Danny got tired enough
to stop. He would play as hard as he could then suddenly
stop, exhausted. It wasn't long before he collapsed on
Gabe's chest.

"Give up?" Gabe asked.

"No," Danny said, but he just lay there, his little
chest going up and down.

Gabe tickled Danny again. But when he didn't respond, Gabe stopped. "I'm thirsty," he said. "Time for
a water break."

"Me thirsty, too," Danny said without moving.

Gabe sat up and set Danny next to him. "How about
some orange juice?"

"Juice," Danny said.

Dana started to mention the coffee cooling on the table next to her then changed her mind.

Gabe stood up. "You're a mess," he told Danny.
"Your shirttail is out."

"Yours, too," Danny said.

"I'll have to fix that." He stood and tucked his shirttail in. Danny got to his feet and tried to do the same
thing. Gabe had to help him. "Ready for that juice?"
Gabe asked.

"Yup," Danny replied.

The two of them headed off to the kitchen, Danny
doing his best to match his steps to Gabe's.

If she hadn't seen it, she wouldn't have believed it,
but wrestling in the floor had accomplished something
nothing else had. Clearly little boys needed dads. When
that was impossible, a kind uncle would do.

But what about little girls?

It had been a long time since Dana had asked herself that question. Nothing she did—had ever done—managed to capture her father's attention for more than a few minutes. He paid the most outrageous bills for college, clothes, travel, anything she wanted, without a blink as long as it left him free to focus all his attention on what he loved most, the job of making money. His wife didn't appear to want or need anything else from him. He didn't understand why Dana should be any different.

So Dana had told herself she didn't want anything, didn't need anything, could do quite well by herself. And she had. Making shameless use of every contact she'd ever made in school, college and summer vacations, she worked tirelessly to build her antique business into one of the most important firms in the New York area. Finally her father noticed. His praise made her so happy she devoted even more time to her job, hoping for more praise, more attention.

When Mattie had come to live with her, she needed support in the aftermath of learning she was pregnant, being deserted by her lover and discovering she couldn't go home. Next came the preparations for Danny's birth, the first months afterward, the last terrible month of Mattie's illness. Sometime during those three years Dana's business ceased to be the center of her life. As Mattie's crisis approached, Dana's business actually became an unwanted intrusion.

During Danny's illness she'd virtually ignored it.

Now all of her responsibilities were about to come to an end. She would be free to devote all her time once more to her work. Her partner would be happy. Her parents would be happy. She ought to be happy.

So why wasn't she?

Chapter Ten

Gabe woke with a start. He raised himself on his elbow then fell back on the bed. He'd been having another dream. It might as well have been a nightmare. It drained him just as completely. He'd been making love to Dana…rather he'd been *trying* to make love to her. But every time he got close, held her in his arms and lay down on the bed next to her, the dream would shift and she'd be out of range again. It seemed the harder he tried, the more quickly she moved away.

Escaped was probably a better word. It's certainly what she would have done if he'd really tried to make love to her.

A film of perspiration covered his body. The sheets stuck to his back, the pillow to his cheek. He rolled over and looked at the clock—2:37 a.m. and he hadn't gotten a half an hour's good sleep. He'd be so groggy tomorrow he wouldn't be safe to be around. He'd have to avoid machinery, stick to sanding and varnishing.

If he didn't mess that up.

He blamed it all on Dana. If she weren't sleeping on the other side of that wall, if she weren't such a beautiful, desirable woman, he wouldn't be lying awake suffering the tortures of the damned. Of course, he had to accept some blame. Only a fool would let himself get this worked up over a woman he knew he couldn't have. A woman he shouldn't even want.

No, he couldn't buy that. He and Dana had their differences, but she was certainly a woman worth having. She just wasn't the woman for him. She'd been cute and fun even as a little girl. But she remained too far distant in age, preference and worldly situation to be more than a visitor in their small community.

Even after he stopped blaming her for keeping Mattie from coming home, from trying to make peace in the family, he knew Dana was the wrong woman for him. She could never fit into his life. No matter how much he might love her, or she him, he would lose her, just like Ellen. He'd lost too much already—his sister, his father, his wife. He'd never wanted to take a chance on losing again.

Then three days ago Dana walked back into his life, and everything changed.

She wasn't a girl anymore. Nothing about her said she was too young, too innocent. She had developed into a woman in her gorgeous prime, with a great body and a style of clothing that accentuated every nice curve and line she had. And she had a lot. He didn't dare allow himself to count them. He'd done that last night when he couldn't sleep. After half an hour, he'd had to get up and take a cold shower.

He could have survived his physical reaction to her better if she'd been the spoiled, selfish, temperamental, success-driven female shark he'd made her out to be. She wasn't anything like that. With that realization, his wall of defense started to crumble.

She'd been a steadfast friend to Mattie. Not many people would have taken his sister in when she was pregnant and made her child a part of their life. Not even Gabe's prejudice could deny that Dana truly loved Danny. That had been the last and greatest breach in his defenses. No woman who could love Danny as much as she did could be all bad. He could only guess how hard it must be for her to give him up. Yet she was doing her best to allow him to build a relationship with Danny.

Now that was a woman of character, a woman a man could admire.

Only he didn't want to admire her. He especially didn't want to like her. And he'd best remember she was a confirmed career woman, independent and opinionated as all get-out. She had only consented to be married temporarily, to keep Danny from being given to his natural father. She hadn't shown any desire to marry Gabe or any interest in the kind of life he could give her.

He flipped over in the bed. He hated sticky sheets. Maybe if he put the air conditioner on and lowered the thermostat to fifty, he could at least keep dry. Maybe, but he'd probably give Danny pneumonia.

He sat up in bed. This wasn't working, but he couldn't move out. That would blow the whole scheme. If he explained his desperation, maybe Matt would give him some sleeping pills.

No, he couldn't explain anything to anybody, not even to the family doctor. If only his marriage wasn't a pretense.... That thought sent his temperature back through

the roof. Why did he even think that? Dana didn't want
to marry him. He didn't want to marry Dana.

Did he?

No, but that didn't stop him from feeling like he was
being turned on a spit. With a muttered curse, he got out
of bed. He fumbled in the drawer for dry underwear.
He'd take a shower. If that didn't work, maybe he'd go
for a walk. He stepped out into the hall and came face-
to-face with Dana.

"What are you doing up?" she asked. Shock showed
in her face, sounded in her voice.

"I couldn't sleep."

Moonlight poured in from one end of the long hall,
from the other came light from the street lamp. Neither
was very strong, but they were quite sufficient for Gabe
to see Dana wore baby-doll pajamas made from a nearly
sheer material. He thought he could see the dark brown
circle of her nipples.

Her presence had an immediate effect on his body.
Only then did he remember he was wearing a pair of
jockey shorts *and nothing else.* He had about ten seconds
before his condition would be easily visible even in the
dim light.

"Neither could I. I thought I'd get a drink of water,"
she said.

"There's ice water in the fridge."

"It's not good for you to drink ice water in the middle
of the night."

It would be good for him.

"What were you going to do?" she asked.

He casually tried to position the dry clothes strategi-
cally. He couldn't tell her he needed a cold shower.
She'd know why. "I sweated through my underclothes.

I need another shower.'' He started backing toward his room. "You go first. Just yell when you're done.''

"It'll only take a second.''

"I'll wait.''

He ducked inside his bedroom. Sweat had broken out on his forehead. His temperature had risen at least ten degrees. His body was as hard as a rock and miserably uncomfortable. He kept visualizing Dana in those damned baby-doll pajamas. Hell, she might as well have been naked. If she had been even half as nervous he was, she didn't show it. So much for thinking himself the man of the world and her the naive little girl he had to protect. It looked as if he was the one who needed protection. Or at least help. A little more of this, and he would be a basket case.

Maybe if he spent less time with Danny he wouldn't think about her so much. No. If he did that, he couldn't build the rapport with Danny he wanted. But he had to come up with something. He'd never survive two months of this.

"I'm done,'' Dana called. She stood in the doorway to his room, her image as tantalizing as before.

"Maybe you should think about having that bathroom put in,'' she said.

"I'll see about it first thing tomorrow.'' But that wouldn't help as long as she wandered about half-nude.

"Well good night.''

"Night.''

He waited until he heard the door to her room close. Then he went straight to the shower and turned the cold water on full force.

But that didn't solve the problem any more than the short walk afterward. He returned to his bed as hot and restless as before. The longer he tossed and turned, the more irritable he became. He felt cornered, with nowhere to go. He felt intruded on. His home, his sanctuary had been invaded, taken over, turned into a torture chamber instead of a place to relax and unwind. He felt resentful, stressed out and sexually frustrated. And for the time being he didn't see any way out.

Dana listened to the silence of the big house and felt very much alone. Gabe had gone to the shop before she got up. He'd left a note saying he'd fallen behind in his work and wouldn't be home until late. It hadn't surprised her. Mattie said Gabe was a slave to his work. It did surprise her that she missed having him at the table. So did Danny.

''Where Gabe?''

If he'd asked that once, he'd asked it a dozen times before he managed to finish his breakfast. She'd had to scramble an egg. Cereal wouldn't do anymore. She managed to avoid the bacon, but she suspected Danny knew she'd left something out. He'd probably figure out what by tomorrow morning, and she'd been in for a high cholesterol breakfast for the rest of her marriage.

That word hit her like a brick. She was married. Even though they both intended it to be temporary. Gabe was her husband. Legally she was Mrs. Gabriel Purvis.

She'd keep her name. That would raise a lot of eyebrows in town, but not half as many as their divorce. She and Gabe had decided it would be best never to tell anyone that the marriage had been arranged. Just let them think things had gone as badly as with Gabe's first marriage. It bothered her to have him bear the onus of the divorce, but he'd insisted he wanted it that way.

She'd spent the first hour after dropping Danny off at day care doing their laundry and straightening up their rooms. She'd never done that before—either Mattie or the cleaning service had always taken care of it for her—but she found an unexpected sense of satisfaction in the work. She couldn't recall the last time she'd made her bed, but she never considered leaving Gabe's bed unmade. She'd looked in his bedroom after he'd gone. You couldn't tell anyone had used it. He'd even put his shoes in the closet.

Just touching Gabe's clothes seemed to forge an intimate connection between them. Whether socks, work pants, or underclothes, the effect remained unchanged. She knew she was being silly, but her body refused to be sensible. By the time she got everything sorted, washed and in the dryer, she felt exhausted. He'd have to fold them and put them away himself.

Looking into the various rooms of the house, even straightening up, made her self-conscious. She couldn't forget she was in Gabe's house, using his things. The connection grew stronger by the minute.

In all the years she'd spent dating other men, twice coming close to being engaged, she'd never given much thought to what a difficult adjustment marriage must be. She had discussed where to live, how to mesh careers, where to spend Christmas vacation, but never the little things that struck her with such force now. Bedspreads and curtains that didn't match. Towels and shower curtains of different colors. The choice of where to place rugs, hang pictures, arrange furniture.

It must be difficult for one partner to move into the other partner's house. One would feel intruded on, the other feel slightly out of place. But at least they had love to hold them together, the knowledge that they were making decisions, sacrifices, compromises toward building the foundation of their future together.

She had none of that in this marriage of convenience. She could only compare it to an extended hotel stay. She might rearrange a few things to make it more comfortable, but nothing really mattered because it wouldn't last.

Every room of the house seemed to repeat that message like a mantra. Gabe's furniture seemed to accuse her most loudly. These were the solid, often unadorned, functional, possessions of a man's life—furniture created for real people, to be beautiful as well as serve a purpose, not something ornamental or designed to draw attention. Everything seemed to say that this was real, that her antiques were only art forms reflecting fickle fashion, imitations of life, only skimming the surface.

Dana retreated to the den, the room least identified with Gabe. Except for the deer's head above the fireplace. Why did he have to desecrate the lovely walnut surround with the head of a dead animal? She tried to read, but she couldn't concentrate. That animal stared at her out of lifeless eyes. She straightened the room twice, straightened it a third time to restore it to the way Gabe had it when she moved in. But she couldn't get her mind off that hideous head. Finally she couldn't stand it any longer. She would go to Gabe and ask him to let her remove it.

Making that decision relieved the pressure. At first she thought it was due to the hope she could talk Gabe into taking the head down, at least until she returned to New York. Next she thought her feeling of relief might be due to getting out of the house. Until she'd come to Iron Springs, she never had time to sit still and do nothing. She didn't have a real link to anybody in this town except Gabe. She felt like a stranger in the midst of a family reunion.

She had no difficulty finding the shop. But having reached the door, she hesitated. She wondered if Gabe would feel she had invaded another part of his life. Maybe, but he would have to get used to it. She had every intention of being a constant in his life until Danny went off to college.

The familiar smells of wood, dust, varnish, stains, paint, the contents of so many shops she visited in connection with restoring antiques, made her feel more at ease than any time since she'd been in Iron Springs. The scream of a saw died away as three men looked up from their work.

"What are you doing here?" Gabe asked.

She hoped she didn't look as uncomfortable as she felt. "I've never seen your shop. I thought I'd come down and let you show me what you do."

She didn't know either of the men working with Gabe, but they stared at her as if they'd never seen a woman before. She guessed no female had dared invade their private world.

"I spent a large part of the morning admiring your work, especially the carving on that ball-footed table," she said. "I wanted to see how you did it."

"Billy did that," Gabe said. "You'll have to tell him what you think of it. Come here, Billy. Dana wants to see you."

A short, thin man with the face of a teenager blushed before he stepped forward a couple of steps.

"Did you do that table?" Dana asked.

He nodded.

"It's beautiful."

"Billy's the best carver in the state," Gabe said.

"I don't do all the carving," Billy said, looking at the floor as he spoke. "Gabe does a lot of it."

"Just the easy stuff," Gabe said. "I make Billy do all the really flashy stuff."

"You're very good," Dana said, surprised such a modest man could carve such bold figures. "Did you do the cherubs?"

"Gabe did those. I like lions and eagles, that kind of stuff."

"What about the angels?"

"Gabe did those, too," the other man said. He winked at Dana. "Billy would get so upset working on a female body he'd probably carve a chunk out of himself."

The fiery red color of Billy's complexion supported the man's statement, but Dana was more surprised at Gabe. How could a man who could carve such a beautiful angel, cherubs with truly beatific expressions, mount a deer head where he had to look at it every day?

"What do you do?" she said, turning to the other man.

"That's Sam," Gabe said, "the most unregenerate jokester in Iron Springs. When I can get him to pay attention to his work, he's a top-notch joiner. He can fit two pieces of wood together so precisely you can hardly see the joint."

"That's because Gabe puts on enough layers of stain and varnish and shellac to cover a quarter-inch gap."

"I wouldn't want you to lose your reputation," Gabe said.

"And what do you do?" Dana asked Gabe.

"I design the pieces."

"He tells the customers what they *really* want," Sam said. "You wouldn't believe some of the fool things people ask for. Gabe makes sure they get something we can be proud of."

"Them, too," Gabe added.

The hardest part of Dana's job was talking customers into making good choices. She had a lot of respect for anyone who could do it.

"He does all the finishing, too," Sam said. "He won't trust us near a piece once we've done our part."

"It's not as bad as that," Gabe said.

"Yes, it is," Billy managed to say. "And a good thing, too. Neither one of us could do it as well as Gabe."

"You don't have the patience to keep at it until you get it right," Gabe said.

"Do you have any pieces you're finishing now?" Dana asked. "All I see are parts."

"That's in another room," Sam said. "He just popped in to make sure we weren't doing anything wrong while he wasn't here to watch us."

"Come on, I'll show you," Gabe said. "If I listen to much more of this, I'll have to fire them."

He showed her into a room with several pieces at or nearing completion.

"You've practically got a factory here."

"There aren't enough people in the area to buy up all the pieces we make. So we make extra pieces and sell them to outsiders."

"Like who?" She didn't know anyone who actually bought handcrafted furniture.

"I sell a few pieces in Harrisonburg and Charlottesville. I've got a buyer coming from Middleburg in a few days."

"How much do you generally get for a piece?"

"That corner cabinet might go for two thousand," he said, pointing to a beautiful cabinet with scroll work and fluted columns.

"I could sell it for at least twice that amount," she said. "Three times that if I found the right customer."

"Don't tell Sam. He'll pack up the shop and head north tonight."

Dana had recognized Gabe's talent when she saw the grandfather clock. Somehow seeing the pieces raw, unfinished, only half-constructed, brought home its magnitude. "You realize you're brilliant, don't you?" For the first time since she'd known him, Dana had managed to throw Gabe off balance. It showed in his face, his averted gaze.

"I just make furniture. People tell me what they want, and I come up with an idea for—"

"That's just it," Dana said, "it's your ideas. Anybody can make furniture. A few can even make it as well as you do. But I haven't seen anyone producing pieces of such character and individuality. You're making the antiques of the future. Now tell me how you come up with your designs."

After seeing Dana home, Gabe returned to the shop in a daze. Dana hadn't just said nice things about his work. She *meant* them. He'd been tempted to pass them off as an effort to make conversation, but Dana always said what she thought, even when she shouldn't.

And she knew furniture.

Delighted to have someone besides Sam and Billy who knew something beyond the basics of what he did, he'd talked about things he'd done, what he was doing, what he hoped to do, pieces that failed to meet his expectations, even the history of a few pieces for which he had managed to find owners able to appreciate his work. He'd been stunned when, after he finally came to halt, he found he'd been talking more than two hours. Equally astounding, Dana had listened. Her questions had proved that.

"You trying to drive her back to New York?" Sam asked when Gabe returned to the workshop.

"What did you talk about?" Billy asked.

"Furniture," Gabe said, "the whole time. She knows as much as I do."

"How come?" Sam asked.

"She owns an antique business."

He'd thought all she had to do to sell antiques in New York was know something about periods, styles, the names of a few famous makers, look beautiful and have lots of friends in the social register. Dana not only understood furniture and its design, she understood why he put a piece together one way and not another. Not even Sam and Billy understood that most of the time. Nobody in Iron Springs had a clue.

He couldn't stop grinning. He probably looked like a fool, but he felt good through and through, equally as good as he had been miserable this morning. He had found someone who could really understand his work. This was something he'd never had with Ellen. Not even his family. Up until now he'd felt spiritually isolated.

He refused to let reality steal the warmth from his happiness. He'd enjoy it just like it would last forever.

The food was dry and tasteless. She'd worked hard to fix this dinner, the first full meal she'd cooked in her whole life, and Gabe had been late. He had called, but he waited until five minutes before she expected him home, too late to do anything but put everything on low and let it simmer.

She'd simmered, too. Every minute she waited, she got a little more angry, remembered a few more instances when he'd done something to irritate her. Now he sat across the table, calmly eating, as though nothing was wrong. He made a game out of feeding Danny. Neither one appeared to sense she was upset. Men! Insensitive, unobservant and uncaring. It seemed no male was too young to be afflicted.

"Want some dessert?" she asked.

"I'm full," Gabe said as he lifted Danny from his high chair. "Find the trains. I'll be in as soon as I help Dana with the dishes."

"Danny want red train."

"You'd better hide it," Gabe called. "I'm going to steal it when I come in." They heard Danny scrambling around in the den. "That ought to hold him for a few minutes," Gabe said. "Now tell me what's eating you."

"Nothing is *eating* me. Why should it be?" she continued, slamming a plate down on the counter so hard she was surprised it didn't break. "The dinner I worked an hour to fix was only ruined."

"It tasted fine."

"It sat in the oven, drying out for thirty minutes. It couldn't be fine."

She heard her voice raised perilously close to a shout. She forced herself to be calm. She would not demean herself by hollering at him. "I expected you to be home at six-thirty. That's what you said. I planned to have dinner ready at that time."

"I'm sorry, but I can't stop in the middle of a project."

"You could have called."

"I did."

"Five minutes before you were supposed to be here. It didn't do any good then."

"I'm sorry."

"I bet you wouldn't do that to your mother."

"My dad was late all the time. Women here learn to work around it."

Now he was telling her she wasn't as good as the women in Iron Springs. "You could have told me that years ago."

"Why? What? When?"

"It would have been better than all that nonsense about us being too far apart in age, not being on the same social level, not having any interests in common."

"What are you talking about?"

She couldn't believe he couldn't remember. Not even he could be that insensitive. "If you can't remember, I'm not going to—"

"Are you talking about that night you told me you'd been in love with me since you were eleven?"

She refused to dignify that with an answer. She grabbed up a bowl and scraped the remaining broccoli spear into the garbage disposal.

"What has that got to do with being late for dinner?" he demanded.

"It just proves you're just as insensitive as you were then."

"Insensitive? I racked my brain to find a way to let you down without hurting your feelings."

She whirled on him. "Do you call saying you couldn't afford to buy my clothes, that I'd be embarrassed to introduce my husband to my fancy friends a sensitive response?"

"I'd never had a child, especially one whose father was a millionaire, beg me to ditch my fiancée and marry her. I was a little out of my depth."

"I wasn't a child. I was a teenager. Half the women in Iron Springs are married by the time they're fifteen."

"What was I supposed to say?"

"It's too late now."

"Tell me anyway."

There really wasn't anything he could have said. She'd been planning to marry him for years. She had made Mattie spend hours talking about him, telling her everything he liked—food, television programs, colors, music, even which side of bed he slept on. She hadn't even known he was dating anyone, much less thinking about getting married. She probably wouldn't have done anything as appalling as ask him to break his engagement if the news hadn't been such a shock.

It was an even worse shock to realize he'd never been able to see beyond her looks, social position and her father's money. The real Dana Marsh had remained a shadow he couldn't see.

He still couldn't.

"There's no particular thing you should have said," she said, evasively. "You just should have been more sensitive, mature enough to understand."

"I supposed you were sensitive and mature when you turned around and talked Mattie into going off to college with you instead of here in the valley."

"Grandmother told me to offer her a scholarship. I didn't think Mattie would take it, but grandmother insisted. I was surprised when Mattie practically jumped at the chance. I won't tell you I wasn't delighted. Mattie was a brilliant artist. If she'd lived, she'd have made as much of a name for herself in fabrics as you will in furniture."

He looked stunned as though someone had hit him from behind. "It was your grandmother's idea?"

"You thought it was mine?"

He nodded.

"I was sixteen, remember. All I could think about was marrying you. It never occurred to me to worry about Mattie's career."

"Why would your grandmother do such a thing? She had to know what it would do to our family."

"Grandmother didn't like what your father was doing to Mattie. She said a parent ought to give children the right to stretch their wings, to soar as high as they could. Then when they decided where to come down, they'd be happy because it would be a place of their own choosing. She said your father didn't care about girls, that he thought of them as pieces of property to marry off and to give him grandsons."

"Mattie's leaving broke my mother's heart," Gabe said, his voice flat, emotionless. "Do you know what it's like for a woman to be forced to choose between her husband and her only daughter?"

"You can't blame me for that. I bet you hold me responsible for her getting pregnant, too."

"Don't be ridiculous."

"I'm not. If I hadn't talked her into going away, she wouldn't have met Lucius and fallen in love with him."

He didn't answer.

"You obviously didn't know your sister as well as you thought. She wouldn't have stayed here even if my grandmother hadn't offered her a scholarship. She had already started applying for scholarships. Grandmother knew because Mattie asked her for a character reference. Mattie didn't dislike Iron Springs, and she didn't hate her father. She just wanted her own life."

They'd strayed so far from the original point of their argument, she wasn't angry about dinner anymore. It really hadn't been ruined. But after all that work, planning to surprise Gabe, anticipating pleasing him, maybe even getting a kind word, her emotions were on a very short leash.

"And you thought my reaction was insensitive," Gabe said. "What was I supposed to say when you talked of nothing but your career, how you were going to be such a great success you'd impress your parents. You had everything mapped out. You even knew when you were going to have children, how many, what sex, where they would go to school, what your husband would do, where you would live, the kind of cars you would drive—"

"I was a young girl," she interrupted, embarrassed. "Those were dreams. I didn't know what I was talking about."

The picture he painted shocked her. She hadn't been thinking about the material things. She'd been talking about home, family, friends, being surrounded by the love she'd never had.

"I suppose you also thought I agreed with everything my father did," Gabe said.

"I don't know what you thought."

"Because you never came back after that summer. Considering what you said about Iron Springs that night, I wasn't surprised."

She colored. Hurt had made her say things she didn't mean, had never even thought. But she had felt so betrayed, so let down, she couldn't help it. The one man she thought understood her had turned out to be just like everybody else.

"I didn't mean that."

"But you meant what you said when it came to thinking you were in love?"

"Okay, so maybe I wasn't being realistic. That didn't change the way I felt. Or thought I felt."

She had been too young, too naive, to know what she really wanted. She'd talked about clothes, school and success when all she really wanted was love, attention, to feel valued. If she had been able to tell him of her need, he probably wouldn't have believed it. He couldn't see the real Dana because she didn't know how to show it to him. Why had it taken her so long to see this?

Because Mattie and all the unhappiness surrounding her stood between them. Dana had felt as though she'd had to defend Mattie against her family. Gabe had thought she'd wanted to separate Mattie from her family. They had squared off against each other, each determined not to give an inch, and Mattie had let them.

"Mattie didn't want me to see you when I came to New York," Gabe said.

So he hadn't avoided her. She supposed it didn't make any difference now, but it made her feel better.

"I didn't stay away from Iron Springs because I hated you. After grandmother died, I didn't have any reason to come back. Mattie said it would just cause trouble."

She stood there looking at him, wondering. She probably hadn't loved him back then. She was too young to understand what love was about. Maybe he had been too surprised by her impassioned declaration to think before he spoke. She didn't know. She had been too hurt that he couldn't give her the love she wanted to understand anything beyond the fact he'd refused her for another woman.

"What happened with your marriage?" She'd always wanted to know.

"She didn't want to live in Iron Springs."

"Surely you knew that before."

"We agreed to try it, to see if she could learn to like it."

"And?"

He hesitated. "She didn't want any children. Without telling me, she got her tubes tied just before we got married."

If Ellen had known anything about Gabe, she must have understood how he felt about having a family.

Dana knew. "I'm sorry."

"I should have told you when I proposed this sham wedding."

"You mad at Danie?" Danny stood in the doorway, confusion and uncertainty taking the sweetness from his expression. Dana had no idea how long he had been standing there.

"No, I'm not mad at Dana," Gabe said.

"You hollered. Mama says hollering makes people cry."

"Well, I'm not crying," Dana assured him. She knelt down and gave him a reassuring hug. "Did you hide the train from Gabe?" She didn't know how to explain away the argument. She knew Danny wouldn't forget it—children never forgot anything that threatened their security—so she decided to get his mind on something else.

Danny nodded. He glanced at Gabe, a smile peeping out from behind threatening tears.

"I bet I can find it," Gabe said.

"Can't," Danny said.

"Bet I can."

Danny cast a questioning look back at Dana, then let himself be lured back into the den. Dana went back to cleaning up, her irritation over the spoiled dinner completely gone.

As stupid as it seemed now, she'd always assumed Gabe was mad at her because of the uncharitable things she'd said to him the night she told him she had been planning marry him since she was eleven. He hadn't known how to handle her confession any more than she'd known how to handle her rejection.

She hadn't known he held her responsible for the rift in his family. He hadn't known his sister very well if he thought anybody could tell Mattie what to do. Dana had learned that before they were six. Now that he knew the truth, he might even be grateful for what she'd done. At least he might not be angry at her. He might even learn to like her.

She had to admit she'd been just as blind, as determined she was right, that he was entirely wrong. She'd never tried to think of anything from his perspective. What could he have done to keep from hurting the pride of a sixteen-year-old girl who'd had nearly everything she'd ever wanted except to be loved by the people most important to her?

It had taken her a long time to realize she wasn't so much angry at his refusing to marry her as his not loving her, something she wanted desperately. She wanted a substitute for her parents who'd always had something more important to do than be with their daughter. She'd settled on Gabe as the person to fill that need. When he hadn't, she'd been unable to forgive him.

Now that she had, she hardly knew what she did feel about him. Or her marriage. But did it make any difference? He still thought of her in terms of New York, her success, her money. He still didn't know the real Dana.

Did she? After the happenings of the last few days, she was beginning to wonder.

The top row of blocks tumbled off the train. ''You've got too many on there, little fella,'' Gabe said to Danny. ''You'll have to make another trip.''

They'd compromised. They both played with the train, each taking a turn transferring everything in Danny's toy box from one side of the room to the other. They'd built a fort, a castle and a zoo for all of Danny's animals. Now they were carrying everything back across the room. Gabe's knees were killing him. He hadn't spent so much time on the floor since he replaced his mother's old pine floors with oak.

He hadn't been much of a playmate tonight. He couldn't get his conversation with Dana out of his mind. Now he couldn't be sure what he felt.

Though he'd stopped blaming her for standing be-tween Mattie and her family, he'd always blamed her for talking Mattie into leave home. If he believed what she said, nothing either of them did could have made any difference. Mattie would have found a way to leave even without Dana's help.

Why hadn't he understood his sister better?

Mattie had told him she wouldn't talk to their father because it wouldn't change anything. She threatened to refuse to see Gabe if he kept trying to change her mind, lecture her, tell her what to do. She'd told him to go back to Iron Springs and forget he had a sister. Had she also wanted to keep him and Dana apart?

"Gabe, your turn!"

He came out of his abstraction long enough to find Danny had unloaded his blocks and was waiting for Gabe to take his turn with the train. Gabe would have been happy to let Danny have the train all to himself, but taking turns was part of the game.

"What do you want to take next?" he asked.

"Animals," Danny chirped.

But as he loaded the giraffes, leaning their long necks against the lions so they wouldn't fall out of the train,

Gabe's thoughts turned back to Mattie. He knew she'd wanted to go to school to be an artist, but their father had said that was out of the question. He'd said she could practice her *drawing,* but she had to marry Orson. With their mother's intervention, their father had agreed to let Mattie go to a local college. Mattie hadn't argued, so Gabe had assumed she'd accepted their father's decision.

He hadn't been living at home then, but he still should have remembered that, even as a little girl, Mattie had been very determined to get what she wanted. She'd probably have found another way to leave home. Her applying for scholarships proved that.

All the blame he'd pinned on Dana had suddenly been washed away. So where did that leave him? He didn't know. He had to start all over again.

He couldn't decide whether that excited or frightened him. The enormous attraction between them had been manageable when he could still hold her at least partially responsible for what had happened to his family. Everything looked different now. He couldn't be certain what his unruly feelings would do. Already they'd caused him sleepless nights, with thoughts of a future that included Dana. That had been out of the question before. What about now?

Chapter Eleven

W as she merely running away? Dana asked herself the following morning as she waited in her grandmother's house for the carpenter. Ever since last night's talk, the thought of being Gabe's *real* wife had started her questioning beliefs she'd considered bedrock. Desperately in need of a calming influence, she had thought of her grandmother.

She admitted that being in Iron Springs with Danny and Gabe made her career seem less important than at any time during the past ten years. Yet it seemed ridiculous that she could like Gabe just because he made her think of the summers she spent at the farm. Maybe he represented the personal freedom and fulfillment she'd found so elusive. He had done exactly what he wanted without worrying what other people thought. After trying to please people all her life—parents, teachers, customers—Dana found that enormously appealing. New York seemed distant, the pressures of her business vague, even unimportant. The quiet, the stillness, acted on her like a release mechanism. Pressures let go; ideas she'd once thought fundamental fell away, exposed as shallow and meaningless; some things she'd thought essential to her happiness suddenly seemed trivial; needs she'd denied, truths she'd refused to acknowledge, rose to their full importance, demanded attention at long last.

She climbed the steps to the front porch, turned and looked out over the hills and valley below. How many times had she and her grandmother sat out here sharing thoughts so random they might have been snatched out of the ambient air. She'd never realized how important those times had been, how much she missed them after her grandmother's stroke. After her death, it hadn't seemed possible to come back. The memories were too close.

She'd gone to college and started her career.

Somewhere along the way she'd lost her connection to this place. She wondered if she could get it back. The sound of a truck coming slowly up the lane warned her the carpenter had arrived.

A heavyset man of about fifty got out of the truck. Dana didn't remember Mr. Bledsoe, but Gabe had said he was the best in the area.

"Hannah said you'd grown up to be right pretty," he said, giving her a thorough inspection. "She fell shy of the mark."

"Do you open negotiations with all your female customers with flattery?" Dana asked.

He grinned. "It starts things out on a better foot." He looked up at the house. "Glad to see you're thinking about doing something to this place. It's a grand old house. It would be a terrible waste to let it go to ruin."

"I'm depending on you to make it ready to live in."

"You planning to sell? If you are, I know—"

"I'm going to keep it myself."

"Now why would a woman like you want to do a thing like that?"

Leave it to country folk not to beat around the bush. If they want to know something, they just up and ask.

"A lot of reasons." She opened her mouth to say she needed a place to stay when she came down to visit Danny, but realized he'd think that peculiar since she was married to Gabe and saw Danny all the time. "It's taken me too long to learn to appreciate my grandmother. Fixing up the house will help make up for lost time."

"We miss her. Sarah Ebberling was a grand lady. They don't make them like her anymore. She wasn't easy on people, but she had a kind heart."

Dana realized that in all the time she'd spent with her grandmother, she'd never once criticized her daughter for leaving home. She couldn't have been happy that she never came back, but she'd realized it was up to her daughter to make her own life. Dana wondered if her grandmother had tried to explain that to Mr. Purvis. Or whether her giving Mattie the scholarship was an admission he would never understand.

But where did Dana belong? She thought she hated Iron Springs and had included the town in her anger and hurt at Gabe's rejection. She'd certainly included the people for rejecting Mattie.

As Mr. Bledsoe completed his inspection and drove off, she realized she wanted this farm for more than a place to stay when she visited Danny. Having come back to this house and having reconnected with a part of the past she'd so foolishly forgotten, she didn't want to lose it again. The farm gave her a sense of peace, a feeling of belonging she hadn't had since she left. She understood now that her grandmother had been trying to give her the feeling of permanence all children need, the security her parents were too busy to provide.

But she also realized she wouldn't have been able to see it—or understand—if it hadn't been for Gabe. She didn't want to ask why that should be so. She wasn't sure of the answers. Right now she had more than enough questions that had no answers.

Dana disliked the buyer from Middleburg the minute he stepped into Gabe's shop. He obviously didn't think Gabe's furniture warranted his attention. She wondered why he had come.

"Where are the pieces you wanted to show me?" he asked.

"You can look at anything in the shop," Gabe replied. "If I can't sell you a piece, we can make you one just like it."

"Our clientele are extremely selective," he said. "They wouldn't want copies of anything in their home scattered all over the valley."

"Gabe's pieces aren't scattered anywhere," Dana said, trying to keep the irritation from her voice. She could do this. She did it all the time in New York. "Everything he makes is unique. Naturally any piece you ordered would be designed to suit the particular customer and the position the piece will occupy in the client's home."

The buyer turned—rather dramatically, Dana thought—and looked at her much as she expected he would look at a wood beetle. "Who are you?"

"His wife." Her response didn't come as quickly or

as easily as it sounded. The word had caught in her throat. It only tumbled past her tongue because she was so angry at this man.

"And what do you know about fine furniture?"

"Enough to know Gabe makes the best you'll find." She wasn't about to give him the advantage of knowing her background.

"You would naturally feel that way."

"Not all wives are blind to their husband's imperfections."

"Why don't I show you what I have," Gabe said, "and you tell me how close it comes to meeting your requirements."

She couldn't quite interpret the look he gave her. It seemed to be compounded of surprise, amusement and even a little uneasiness that she might drive off a potential customer.

"Why don't I come along," Dana said. "You might want a woman's perspective," she said.

"How could you know what my clients would like?" the buyer inquired.

"Women are women, no matter how much money they have."

The buyer obviously didn't agree but declined to argue the point. Gabe's look still contained surprise and a question, but the amusement had grown more pronounced. She breathed a little easier. He might not want her here, but at least he wouldn't kill her if things went wrong.

For the next hour she followed the two of them from one piece of furniture to another, remaining silent while Gabe told the buyer what the piece was designed to do, why he'd chosen that particular style and design, how he'd put the piece together. Then before the buyer could make any of the disparaging remarks Dana could sense were hovering on his tongue, she launched into a more exhaustive discussion of the style, its usefulness and how it could fit into the various homes and decorating styles found in wealthy estates in the Middleburg area.

"We don't limit ourselves to Middleburg," the buyer said, irritated when Dana had anticipated his criticism of a large and particularly beautiful sideboard.

"Do you get buyers from Washington, D.C.?"

"Why would you want to know that? And anyway, what makes you think you know anything about the taste of people outside this...town."

Dana bristled at the implied slight of Iron Springs. "They let us leave the mountains once in a while. Sometimes they even let us go as far as New York." She sounded like Gabe.

"I doubt that would be sufficient exposure to make you an expert in furniture."

"Some of us mountain folk are fast learners." The man was saying exactly what she'd thought most of her life. But hearing it from someone else, especially this insufferable snob, made her so angry she couldn't control her tongue.

"I'll offer you sixteen hundred for that piece," he said to Gabe, indicating the sideboard.

"It's worth twice that," Dana protested.

"Not to me," the buyer replied. "I'll give you eight hundred now and the rest when it's sold."

"I don't sell on consignment," Gabe said.

"It's the only way I buy handmade pieces," the buyer said. "If my customers like your work, maybe we can work out something else. I want it delivered to my shop within the week. If there are any scratches or imperfections, I won't accept it."

"You won't get that chance," Gabe snapped. "I'm not selling you this piece or anything else. My shop turns out top-quality work. I wouldn't sell anybody anything I wouldn't be proud to put my name on. If you're not equally proud to have it in your store, then I don't want it there."

"If you think you can rob us just because we don't have a showroom in a major city, you've badly mistaken your man this time," Dana said, delighted Gabe had refused to knuckle under to this snob.

"I don't recall that *your* man has said much I can mistake, one way or the other," the buyer said. "What about the chest and tables I wanted?"

"We're not selling you anything," Gabe said.

The buyer looked stunned. Dana couldn't tell whether he was reconsidering his offer or whether he was just too shocked to speak.

"You've heard my offer," he said. "I won't increase it, but I will pay you the entire amount now. I'll also assume responsibility for delivery."

"We have nothing for sale," Gabe said. "Sorry if we wasted your time."

The buyer appeared to consider whether to change his offer but changed his mind. He turned and stalked out of the room. Dana and Gabe followed him to the main room in the shop. He didn't stop to speak to Sam and Billy or say goodbye. He simply walked out.

"Is he crazy?" Sam asked.

"No, just greedy," Dana said. "He thought that he could buy cheap and make a killing."

"He thinks we're stupid rednecks," Billy said.

"Pretty much," Gabe said. "But we set him straight in a hurry. Unfortunately that means we're not going to get any money."

"You know, this stuff is good, *really* good," Dana said. "You can sell it in New York for at least three times what he offered. Everything you make will be collector's items in a hundred years. People would pay thousands for a signed piece. By the way, don't let anything leave this shop without a signature. You'll be famous. You'll be rich."

Gabe laughed. "Don't let that get out, or I'll have everybody dragging me out to their houses to sign their pieces."

"You should. And buy back anything you can."

"With what? Look, all this sounds wonderful, Dana, but we need money to pay the bills."

"You'll get it," Dana said. "I've got contacts all around the country."

Gabe laughed. Then Sam and Billy started laughing. They laughed so hard they could hardly stand up.

"Don't you believe me?" Dana said. Her professional pride was on the line.

"I was remembering how you practically ran that buyer out of the shop," Gabe said.

"I was thinking of being rich," Sam said.

"Do you really think I'll be famous?" Billy asked.

"Yes," Dana said.

"I can buy that new lathe I wanted," Gabe said.

"I'm on my way to pick out my new truck," Sam said.

"What do you want, Billy?" Dana asked.

"I want to go to New York and see something I made in the showroom of one of them fancy shops."

"We can all go to New York," Gabe said. And the three of them started tossing out all the things they wanted to do. Their mood quickly became hilarious.

Suddenly Gabe picked Dana up and whirled her

around. She had to put her arms around his neck to keep from losing her balance.

"She deserves a hug," Billy said, blushing.

"Hug, hell!" Gabe exlaimed. "She deserves a kiss."

Gabe kissed her on the mouth in front of the others.

"You call that lousy peck a kiss?" Sam hooted. "Hell, I can do better than that. If you're aren't up to it, I am."

"I'm up to it," Gabe said.

"What's stopping you?" Sam asked.

"Nothing."

When she looked up at him, the laughter had gone out of his eyes. In its place flamed a heat that suddenly made the shop seem much too small and warm. In the same instant Dana became aware her body was pressing against Gabe, his chin practically between her breasts. He slowly lowered her to her feet, her body sliding down the length of him. Tension exploded inside her with the force of a small bomb. Looking into his eyes warmed her all over. Her toes touched the floor. For a moment they remained motionless, looking at each other.

"Is he going to kiss her?" Billy asked in a whisper.

"Don't know," Sam said. "Maybe he can't remember how."

"I've known how for a long time," Gabe said, his gaze never leaving Dana's face.

"Well nobody could tell it," Sam replied.

"You mind being kissed in front of these clowns?" Gabe asked.

"Of course she doesn't. You've done it once already," Sam pointed out.

Gabe appeared to have lost interest in talking to Sam. The intensity with which his gaze bore into Dana told her he was thinking of no one but her. Suddenly there was no room in her mind for anyone but him.

The kiss was tentative at first, as if he was experimenting to see if she really wanted him to kiss her. Having decided she didn't intend to push him away, he kissed her properly. Too properly. It lacked the passion or the fire Dana saw in his eyes, the passion and fire she felt inside.

She looked into his eyes again but saw caution this time. She put her hand behind his head and pulled him down into a second kiss. She put her whole heart into it. She felt something inside break free, float upward, soar on the wings of a desire that had been kept under wraps for fourteen years.

This kiss had nothing to do with that sixteen-year-old girl or her dewy-eyed worship of an older man. It had to do with a mature woman who had discovered a deep need within herself, a need that only a man like Gabe Purvis could fill.

Gabe reclaimed her lips, crushed her to him. His mouth, hard and greedy, covered hers hungrily. The force of it sent the pit of her belly into a wild swirl. Shivers of desire raced through her, and she kissed him with a hunger that had waited years to be satisfied. When Gabe broke their kiss, he left her breathless.

"That's more like it," Sam said when Gabe set Dana on her feet and stepped back. "I thought for a moment there I was going to have to give you some pointers."

"Gabe doesn't need pointers on how to kiss his own wife," Billy said.

No, Dana thought, he didn't need any pointers at all. But Sam and Billy needed some pointers on when to make themselves scarce.

But then maybe Gabe wouldn't have kissed her without their prompting. At least now she knew Gabe liked her. No man could kiss a woman like that without some strong feelings to back it up.

But should she allow such feelings to exist? Despite the joint custody and the marriage, their relationship would change as soon as they received official custody. It might be good for her ego to know Gabe liked her, but it might complicate their relationship. Regardless of how enjoyable this might be, she ought to be wary.

Chapter Twelve

It had been a nearly perfect day.

Because Mr. Dowd was still trying to convince the judge their marriage was a put-up job, Marshall had urged them to go out, to be seen having fun. He'd even suggested that going to a theme park would be the perfect family outing. So they'd gotten up early, breakfasted together, and whiled away the two-hour drive by identifying animals and counting churches. Once at the park, Danny had ridden nearly every ride, sitting in Dana's or Gabe's lap when necessary, giggling happily when he went high or fast. He positively shrieked with delight when he went high and fast. Dana held her breath on those rides.

Lunch had been hot dogs, cheeseburgers, French fries, soft drinks and a fruit pie, about the only part of the meal Dana considered marginally good nutrition. After an enforced nap—Danny objected to being the only one required to sleep—they had hit the rides again. By the time the park closed, they barely had enough energy to consume another round of fast food, jump in the car and head home. Though she couldn't explain why, that's how Dana felt. She was going home.

"Is he still asleep?" Gabe asked.

Dana glanced down at Danny sound asleep in her arms. "He hasn't moved for the past hour."

"How are you holding up?"

"I haven't been this tired since I stayed up all night setting up a new showroom."

She hadn't thought about her job all day. It reminded her that this tranquil way of living wouldn't last forever.

"I really had a good time today," Gabe said.

"Me, too. I especially enjoyed watching Danny's excitement at all the rides."

"I thought he liked the animals better."

Other things had contributed toward making this a memorable day. She'd enjoyed being with Gabe. Outside of the natural pride of being with the two best-looking men in the park, she found she really enjoyed Gabe's company. They had similar tastes in a lot of ways. They had the same quirky sense of humor, laughed at the same things, understood unspoken jokes. Not even Mattie had seemed to understand Dana's thoughts so well without having to ask.

"Do you think the lawyer spied on us?" she asked.

"Probably. He seems to know everything we do."

Somewhere along the way the day had become so natural, her participation so unconscious, her enjoyment so complete, she'd forgotten about the lawyer. Remembering him now gave her an unwelcome jar. It reminded her that everything they did was a sham.

Yet it hadn't felt that way. She'd almost felt married.

"I wonder what he'll say when I go back to New York?"

"Nothing good."

She didn't want to think about New York. She felt very comfortable with Gabe at her side and Danny in her arms. She couldn't explain exactly what it did for her—she'd never felt this way before—but she wouldn't soon forget the feeling of contentment, of it being so right.

"I'll have to leave soon. I can't expect my partner to continue handling everything by herself."

"I suppose you will."

They were nearing Iron Springs, the road flat and empty. It didn't take any concentration to drive the car. Gabe's response didn't need to be so lifeless. It almost sounded as though he didn't care.

"She's great at organization, but I'm the one who handles most of the sales."

"Your parents must be very proud of your success."

They said so, but next to her father's global enterprises, her business seemed small.

"I'll have to go on a buying trip soon. We're getting low on inventory."

"Where do you go?"

"Anywhere I can find antiques. I went to Argentina last year."

"I'm surprised you could spare this much time."

"Danny is more important than the business."

She'd never actually said that before. But the moment the words were out of her mouth, she knew they were right.

"Then you don't plan to go back right away?"

"No."

"Good."

Gabe pulled the car into the driveway. In the bustle of collecting Danny's stuff and getting him inside without waking him, she didn't have an opportunity to search Gabe's face or gauge the feelings behind his laconic answer. She'd kept mentioning New York, hoping he'd ask her to stay a little longer. She didn't know why that should be so important—she couldn't stay if he asked her—so maybe she wanted recognition of her contribution to Danny's life. Maybe she needed to feel he appreciated her decision to marry him.

All during the day she'd been aware of a difference in the atmosphere between them. She couldn't identify it just yet, but it had enabled them to be much more comfortable, to enjoy being with each other. She felt he wanted her to stay but couldn't say it. Maybe it hurt his pride to admit he had been wrong.

"I want to see if I can get him into bed without waking him," Dana said as she carried Danny into the house. "If he wakes up, he's liable to be up for a couple of hours."

They undressed Danny and got him into his pajamas with only a few mumbled words. As soon as they laid him in the bed, he snuggled down with his teddy bear. Leaving the door open, they tiptoed out into the hall. They paused, looked at each other.

"It was a nice day," Dana said. "I enjoyed myself."

"Me, too."

"You didn't have much to say coming back," Dana said.

"I don't have to deal with the consequences of my words if I don't say them."

"What consequences?"

"The consequences of my saying you're an excep-

tionally beautiful woman. Keeping my hands off you is
nearly driving me crazy.''

His words hit Dana with the force of a fist in the gut.
She'd been feeling pretty much the same about Gabe.

''It's torture every time I have to kiss you,'' he said.

Dana was quite willing to be a temptation. She wasn't
so sure about torture. ''I didn't notice you having such
a hard time staying away.'' She had intended that to
sound like a noncommittal statement. Much to her alarm
it sounded like a complaint. Before she had time to cor-
rect her mistake, Gabe advanced on her, planted his
hands against the wall, pinning her into the narrow space
in between.

''You must know you're a beautiful woman.''

His face was so close she couldn't concentrate on the
whole, just a part. His lips. ''Maybe, but men have never
gone crazy over me.''

''They're fools.''

She laughed. It sounded strained. ''I like to think so,
but their collective wealth could buy half this state.''

''I'd rather be smart about women and stupid about
money.''

''That's not how most men feel.''

''I'm not most men.''

No joke. Nobody else could practically give her heart
failure just by talking to her...being close...looking at
her in a way that said he wanted to make love to her
right then.

''What do you think it's like knowing you're on the
other side of that wall, so close yet out of reach?''

She shook her head.

''Meeting you in the hall with you wearing practically
nothing.''

''You weren't wearing much, either.'' She'd had wild

dreams all night, had awakened feeling as if she hadn't slept at all.

"Knowing you were in my shower…without anything on."

"Nobody takes a shower wearing clothes."

She knew her answers made little sense, but she couldn't concentrate when his lips were so close that she could almost kiss them. This was no posed shot for the cameras, no play-it-by-the-numbers setup for the lawyer. Gabe wanted her, and every fiber of her body wanted him right back.

He kissed her. Considering the heat in his gaze, the intensity of his words, it was surprisingly gentle. Yet the instant she relaxed, his kiss exploded into a huge hunger seemingly intent on devouring her. He covered her mouth with his, the pressure pinning her to the wall. She found herself responding, kissing him back with the same fierceness.

Gabe pushed away from the wall, put his hands on her shoulders and drew her closer to him. She didn't resist when she felt his body against hers. She needed that contact.

"See what I mean?" Gabe said when he finally broke their kiss.

"I don't know what you are so afraid of," she managed to say between deeply drawn breaths. "We've kissed several times before."

"You're not upset?"

"Why should I be?"

Gabe wrapped his arms around her and proceeded to kiss her ruthlessly.

Dana let him.

She doubted she could have stopped him if she'd wanted. The intensity that had seized him erupted inside her. Her arms slipped around his neck, pulled him deeper and deeper into her embrace. Desire that had been held in check for days exploded with a ferocity that overwhelmed her.

He broke their kiss and drew her head down on his chest. He rested his chin on top of her head. It gave her the feeling of smallness, of being cuddled and protected. No one had ever done that. Dana decided she liked it.

She couldn't concentrate when Gabe switched to nibbling her ear. It tickled. At the same time it sent bone-dissolving sensations of weakness all through her limbs. She clung more tightly to him for support.

"Don't do that," she said.

But she didn't mean it, and Gabe knew it. The tip of his tongue traced the shell of her ear. She expected to dissolve right there. She took his head in her hands and kissed him hard.

Gabe's hands wandered over her back, her shoulders, her waist, pulling her against him, setting her skin afire with his touch. When his hands slipped down to cup her bottom and press her body against the hardness of his groin, she teetered on the brink of losing control. It had been a long time since any man had touched her. Her body screamed for release.

Gabe deepened their kiss. Dana couldn't get close enough, couldn't feel enough of his body. She needed more of the hot energy that flowed from him like lava. She was hungry, greedy, demanding, and she—

"Danie."

Dana froze at the sound of Danny's voice.

"Danie! Danny want water."

Dana's body shuddered with released tension. She was certain that if Danny hadn't awakened, she'd have been in bed with Gabe in minutes.

"I've got to go." The force of her passion, cooled with unnatural swiftness, caused her voice to waver. Gabe didn't loosen her hold. "If I don't go, he'll think nobody's here. He'll get upset and start to cry. I'm coming, darling," she called to Danny. "Let me go," she whispered to Gabe.

Gabe released his breath in a single, noisy whoosh. His whole body sagged, and his arms fell to his sides.

"I'm sorry," Dana said as she readjusted her clothes.

"You can't be as sorry as I am," Gabe said. He moved away, turned and walked into his room.

For a moment Dana was too shaken to move. She wanted to apologize, but her thoughts were in chaos. Right now she had to get Danny some water. She would concentrate on that. Once she'd calmed down, she'd try to think. But she already knew one thing.

Everything had changed.

Gabe forced himself to concentrate on the eggs, not on Dana as she moved about the kitchen. They were preparing breakfast, but his thoughts had wandered so far away from cooking he had to keep reminding himself to watch the eggs.

"Want eggs," Danny called from his high chair.

"Coming up, fella," Gabe replied. But when he turned, his gaze fell on Dana, and the blood surged into his loins with painful insistence.

Last night had lowered the barriers. Knowing Dana wanted him as much as he wanted her had unleashed such a torrent of desire Gabe wished it had never happened. The physical attraction this morning had grown so strong it permeated everything they did, thought or said. Every look, every gesture—even the things they

didn't do or say—plucked some string and sent it reso-
nating throughout his body.

 He found himself staring wordlessly at her, certain
that desire danced naked in his eyes. She turned away
from his gaze, avoided him, but it didn't change anything. They both knew what he wanted. They both knew
she wanted it, too. Each time she passed near him, he
wanted to reach out and touch her. Fortunately he
needed both hands to scramble eggs, one to hold the pan
steady and the other to stir. He kept reminding himself
this would only last a few weeks, a couple of months at
most. But if things got much more difficult he would
lose his mind in about three days.

"Do you want milk?" Dana asked.

"Just coffee," he answered.

"Danny want 'coppie,'" Danny said.

"Coffee is for adults," Dana told him.

"Danny 'dult.'"

"You're getting eggs," Dana said. "That's enough
sinning for now."

"What sin? Can Danny have sin?"

Gabe grinned. He couldn't wait to see her get out of
this one.

"That's for adults, too," Dana said. "It's too strong
for little boys."

If wanting Dana was a sin, it was too strong for Gabe,
too. He struggled to get his attention back on the eggs.
They'd be a little dry this morning, but considering the
state of his mind, Danny was lucky they weren't charcoal. It was all Dana's fault. Or his. Either way it re-
sulted in his being practically useless. He would have to
find a way to keep his distance from her.

Maybe he could start staying late at the shop.

No, Dana would be upset, the lawyer would be on

them again, and Danny would already be in bed when he got home. There wouldn't be any buffer between him and Dana.

If he got up at four, he'd be out of the house before she woke up. Then he could go to bed at the same time as Danny. Sam and Billy would think he was nuts for opening the shop in the middle of the night, but that would be better than being in the same room with Dana, desire burning through him like fire through dry timber.

"Heads up," he called. "Here come the eggs."

"I thought I gave you some sausage," Gabe said to Danny.

"He ate it while you scrambled the eggs," Dana said.

"Then we'll just have to give him another piece," Gabe said. Danny picked up the sausage the minute it hit his plate. Dana intercepted it before he could stuff it in his mouth.

"I have to cut it up in small pieces," she said, "I don't want you to choke."

"Danny want choke."

"You'll turn blue and keel over in your chair," Gabe said. He clutched at his throat, pretended he couldn't breathe, then collapsed on the table. Danny crowed with laughter.

"Danny choke." He grabbed his throat, made gagging noises and tilted over in his high chair. He waited a moment, opened his eyes, sat up, and waited for the expected praise. Gabe rewarded him with a laugh.

"Now see what you've done," Dana said. "I'll never understand you men. You do the dumbest things. What I understand even less is why women let you get away with it."

"It's part of our charm."

"It must be. I can't think of any logical reason for it."

"Do you think I'm charming?" he asked. Laughter turned to desire.

"Don't fish for compliments." Color tinged her cheeks. "I'm sure women have flattered you shamelessly for years."

"I don't believe everything I hear."

"I'm sure you'd believe that."

"No more readily than you believe you're attractive."

More color tinged her cheeks. "Do you think I'm attractive?"

"No. I like women with thick legs, huge hips and a nose like a carbuncle."

Dana burst out laughing. "No woman alive would admit to looking like that, not even to catch a prize like you."

The surge of heat through his body threatened to take the little reason left to him. "Do you think I'm a prize?"

"Salome's description," she said, truly blushing this time. "She said I'd gotten a prize in his prime, not to waste it."

Gabe's last shred of self-control vanished into thin air. "Are you going to waste my prime?"

"Danny, you've got eggs all over you, the high chair and the floor," Dana exclaimed. "It's my fault. He always uses his fingers when I'm not watching."

She jumped up to get some paper towels. By the time she'd gathered up all the stray bits of egg and sausage and wiped Danny's mouth despite his objections, she had herself under control.

"I expect your prime will last long past the next few weeks," she said. "I'm sure you will find someone who can put it to good use."

Gabe wondered what she would have said if she'd answered him with the heat still in her cheeks. Before he could ask her, the phone rang.

"I'm sure it's for you, but I'll answer it," she said, getting up before he could object. "You need to finish your breakfast."

When she practically ran out of the room, Gabe felt better. If he had to be broiled like a piece of meat on a rotisserie, he wanted to know he had company.

"I guess it's just you and me, fella," he said, turning to Danny. "Do you think you could keep from making another mess until I can get a straight answer from Dana?"

"Eggs," Danny said pointing at Dana's plate.

"You're a pig," Gabe said as he gave the little boy a bite of his own breakfast. "It's not very gentlemanly to eat a lady's food."

"Sausage," Danny said pointing at the untouched sausage on Dana's plate.

"You planning to eat everything before she gets back?" Maybe the telephone call hadn't been for him. Dana should have been back before now. It was probably her partner wanting to know when she was going back to work. Despite being tied to him by Mattie's will, he'd never expected Dana to stay in Iron Springs more than a few days. Everything she'd wanted from the time she was a little girl was in New York. What could she find in Iron Springs to interest her?

"I'm afraid not even you can keep her here," he said to Danny. "Once they get worldly success in their blood, they're ruined for the likes of us. You don't care what's going on around you as long as I stuff your mouth full of food, do you?" Danny answered by opening his mouth for another bite.

"That's it, fella. Any more and you'll pop. Dana will have a bigger mess than ever to clean up, and she'll blame it on me." He laughed. "Listen to me talking to you like you understand. I wish you did," he said after getting up to take the empty dishes to the sink. "Maybe you could explain it to me."

But he didn't need an explanation. He knew. Despite being made uncomfortable by the intensity of his lust for Dana, he'd been more relaxed and at ease with her than with any other woman he'd known. He'd liked the feeling of having someone to come home to, to talk to about his day, to be able to play with Danny, to help feed him and put him to bed. Having a small, defenseless, dependent child in the house filled a deep need inside him. He *wanted* to play with Danny, feed him, even learn to give him his bath and put him to bed. He *liked* having Dana sitting across the table from him. He liked helping her fix meals, clear away, worry about Danny.

How ironic he should find what he'd wanted for so long in Dana. Of all the women he knew, none could be less likely to fit into his world. And he'd be a fool if he even considered trusting his feelings to her. She wouldn't leave him because she didn't like him; she'd leave because she couldn't do anything else.

He'd already had his heart torn up once. He'd sworn he'd never let it happen again.

Dana came back into the kitchen, her face white. "I've got to leave for New York immediately," she said. "My father's had a heart attack."

That was it. Once she got to New York, she would never leave again. He didn't have to worry about keeping himself from doing something foolish. Her father had done it for him.

Chapter Thirteen

"I don't care if Mattie's will did make you joint custodian of her child," Dana's mother was saying, "there's no reason for you to stay in that godforsaken place a minute longer. I don't understand why you went in the first place."

"I couldn't just turn Danny over to Gabe and leave."

"I don't see why not. He's not your child. He's not even related to you."

"I feel like he's my child," Dana said. "That's why Mattie gave me joint custody. She knew I'd see to it Danny didn't get lost in those mountains."

"She did nothing of the sort," her mother snorted. It was an elegant snort, but it was definitely a snort. "She always wanted to get you and her brother together."

"Don't be ridiculous, Mother. Mattie wouldn't—"

"Everybody knew you were besotted with him when you were a teenager."

Dana blushed. "I got over that long ago."

"Maybe, but Mattie didn't forget it."

"Why would Mattie want me to go back to Iron Springs when she wouldn't go back herself?"

"Maybe she thought you could coax her brother into coming to New York. How am I supposed to know what she thought?"

Dana found herself wishing herself back in Iron Springs. After the doctors declared her father was in no immediate danger, her mother had turned her attention to the aspects of Dana's life she considered unsatisfactory. Dana's friendship with Mattie and her subsequent assumption of responsibility for Danny topped the list.

"You shouldn't let anything keep you from being here with me at your father's side."

Her mother meant that to be the clincher. It might have been if Dana hadn't known her father liked to have his family around him when he was feeling mortal but didn't want to be bothered when he felt fine. She loved both her parents, but that didn't blind her to the fact she wasn't essential to their lives.

"I'll stay as long as Dad needs me," Dana said, "but I have to go back as soon as he's better. I haven't finished teaching Gabe how to take care of Danny. Besides, I still haven't decided what to do with grandmother's house."

"Sell that place," her mother said. "I'm sure the roof is about to fall in. There's nothing out there but trees and field mice."

"I'm going to fix it up so I can stay there when I go to visit Danny."

Both parents looked at her as though she'd taken leave of her senses.

"You're not going back to that place," her father declared.

"I have to."

"No, you don't. That child has his uncle and the rest of his family to look after him. He doesn't need you."

"I'm his joint guardian. I'm responsible for him."

"I can't see any reason—" her mother started.

"I forbid you to go back," her father said. "I'm surprised you'd even consider it."

"Danny's father is trying to get custody."

"I don't see why you shouldn't want the boy's own father to have him," her mother said. "Besides, if the uncle isn't married, there's practically nothing you can do about it."

"I have done something about it," Dana said.

"What?" her father asked. "You don't know any judge. If it were New York, I could—"

"Gabe is married," she said.

"I distinctly remember you telling me he *wasn't* married," her mother said.

"He wasn't married then," Dana said, knowing what had to come sooner or later.

"Who could he have found to marry him on such short notice?" her mother asked.

"Me."

Both parents stared at her in stunned silence. If her father didn't have a fatal heart attack now, he wasn't likely to have one for a very long time.

"The lawyer told us the only way we could keep Danny would be to get married," Dana explained, hoping to take the edge off what she was certain would be a torrent of anger. "He said courts almost always sided with the natural parent. He said we only had to stay married until Gabe had been awarded official custody.

Then we can get a divorce, and I can come back to New York.''

The explosion was worse than she'd expected. Dana let both parents say what they had to say without interruption. She owed them that much.

''I won't divorce Gabe until he has custody of Danny,'' she repeated when they had finished. ''I know you don't like it and you don't understand it, but my mind is made up.''

But the pressure they put on her became intense and unrelenting. When they brought in the family lawyer to convince her to be reasonable, she got on a plane back to Iron Springs.

The minute the plane's wheels left the ground, a weight fell from her shoulders. She could literally feel the tension uncoil inside her. By the time the plane reached cruising altitude, a series of deep breaths had loosened the muscles in her shoulders. When they served beverages she had ceased gripping the seat handle. By the time the plane landed in Virginia, the muscles in the back of her neck had relaxed sufficiently for the pounding headache to pass. She leaned back in her seat, a smile on her lips. Gabe and Danny would be waiting for her.

Gabe spotted her the moment she stepped out of the tunnel. He nudged his mother, pointed her out to Danny. All three broke into huge smiles and waved excitedly.

The smile on Dana's lips turned to marble. With a suddenness that was terrifying, she realized she cared for Gabe. Not the way she'd cared for him as a teenager. She cared for him as a man she lived with, shared meals with, parented with, a man whose thoughts and worries she shared. She cared for him as a woman cares for a man she finds attractive, appealing, desirable.

And that threatened everything she was, that she thought she wanted to be.

Instinct warned her to turn around and run back to New York. Even though she didn't know how to go about doing it, she had to find out if Gabe cared for her, and if so, what she wanted to do about it. Her life had been made up mostly of opposites to his, but regardless of what she did in the future, she knew her career would never be as important as it had been before Mattie came to live with her.

She wouldn't consider giving up everything to become a typical Iron Springs housewife. Yet the appeal of being part of such a loving and supportive community gripped her strongly. Her parents had never met her at the airport nor looked nearly so happy to see her. Neither had any of the men she'd dated. After years of being too busy, of not finding a man who could give her the love and acceptance she craved, of dating men too busy or too uninterested to commit, she'd found a man who'd conquered the citadel of her heart despite the efforts of both of them to keep it from happening.

No matter what the consequences, she had to find out what that meant, she thought as Danny pushed his way through the crowd and threw himself into her outstretched arms. Watching the scene, Gabe wondered if two people could hug each other any harder than Danny and Dana. They hardly seemed to be aware when he and his mother reached them.

Gabe had expected to be relieved Dana had returned. The extent of that relief surprised him. He'd dreamed about her, missed the sight and sound of her moving about the house. He called her every night to report on Danny, but he hadn't expected to feel like a part of him had been restored when she emerged from the tunnel.

No matter how much it frustrated him, he liked having her around. He didn't understand how she could have become such a necessary part of his days so quickly, so easily integrated into his routine, but nothing seemed right without her. Even his mother had commented on the difference.

"Don't take all of Dana's sugar, young man," Mrs. Purvis said to Danny. "Save some for Gabe."

Dana stood to face Gabe, Danny on her hip. Gabe felt very self—conscious. He gave her a little kiss on the cheek.

"You don't have to act like a preacher just because your mother's present," Mrs. Purvis said in disgust. "Here, let me have Danny so you can kiss her good and proper."

Dana hesitated, but Mrs. Purvis took Danny. "You can go back in a minute," she said to Danny when he held out his arms to Dana. "You're going to have to learn to share her from now on. Go on," she prompted when Gabe hesitated. "It isn't like these people never saw a man kiss his wife before."

Giving in to the pressure that had been building to the point of explosion, Gabe took Dana in a two-arm embrace and kissed her. His action had been spontaneous, without plan, but he no sooner had Dana in his arms than he knew exactly what he wanted to do. The kiss deepened until he felt Dana's arms go around his neck. His tongue forced its way into her mouth, searching hers.

Each kiss, each embrace, blew the top off a need he constantly struggled to keep under control. Because he knew the feeling of fulfillment couldn't last long, he was determined to grab every bit of pleasure he could whenever he got the chance. It wasn't a hard decision to make.

Her mouth tasted so sweet, her lips felt so soft, he wanted to keep kissing her forever. When she kissed him back with reckless abandon, he decided he just might. The hunger of her kiss shattered his slender supply of calm. Shivers of barely contained desire rushed through him.

"Gabe."

The kiss was like the soldering heat that joins metals. He took her mouth with savage intensity. Her body quivered its surrender, and he closed in for the—

"Gabe!"

When he released her, Dana didn't move, just stared at him. She looked quite shaken. Gabe didn't know whether positively or negatively, pleased or displeased. He felt weak in the knees.

"If I'd known you were going to make a spectacle of yourself, I'd have told you to wait until you got home," Mrs. Purvis said as she let Danny go back to Dana. "You looked like one of those couples in a movie."

"I just did what came naturally," Gabe said, recovering.

"Well next time maybe you'd *better* act like a preacher."

Gabe winked at Dana. The stunned look had disappeared, and she smiled in return.

"Why don't you ask Dana if she liked it," Gabe said.

"That's none of my business. Now get her luggage. If you don't hurry, you'll be late feeding Danny his dinner."

Gabe headed off to the luggage counter with a light step. Dana was back.

He didn't know how he was going to get through the next few weeks, but he decided not to worry about it.

He'd have to let things happen, he'd worry about tomorrow when it came.

"I didn't know Yankees knew how to cook." Salome said as she helped herself to some chicken salad. "You've got enough food laid out here to serve half of the town."

"She's practically got half the town here," Liz said.

"I don't see Josie Woodhouse," Salome pointed out.

"Josie came to my luncheon," Mrs. Purvis said. "That's enough."

Dana had decided a Saturday morning ladies' brunch would be one of the best ways to appear to be fitting into the community. Mrs. Purvis had made up a sympathetic guest list, and she'd sent Gabe and Danny off to the park with orders to bring home takeout for dinner.

"Mrs. Purvis did most of the work," Dana confessed.

"Dana made the chicken salad and the cucumber sandwiches," Mrs. Purvis said.

"You'll have to give me the recipe for these sandwiches," Liz Dennis said. "I want to serve them the next time Matt has a gathering of his snooty doctors."

The past week had been one of incredible happiness for Dana. Facing pressure from Lucius's lawyer, Marshall had ordered Gabe to come home earlier for dinner and for Dana to become involved in the community. Dana had volunteered for the crafts fair and immediately been put in charge of getting commitments from as many buyers as possible. She'd attended church and volunteered to help in the nursery. That way she wouldn't have to leave Danny.

She also volunteered to spend three mornings a week in the clinic. After her first day with Salome, she had reconsidered the situation. By the third, she had confirmed her original impression that Salome could be a real friend—as long as Dana could manage to close her eyes to Salome's violently clashing colors.

Dana had fallen into the habit of picking up Danny and taking him to share lunch with Gabe. This meant she had to bring something for Billy and Sam, too, but she didn't mind. Fixing soup or salad for five was just as easy as fixing for three.

Danny looked forward to these lunches. Gabe made certain all the machines were off, everything dangerous out of reach. He did his best to answer all of Danny's questions about the machines and the dozens of other tools and pieces of equipment.

Dana looked forward to these times, as well. Gabe had never been so approachable, so at ease, so much like a friendly lover without requiring her to act loverlike. She loved watching the progress of his work almost as much as she enjoyed watching his progress with Danny. He still had a lot to learn about small children, but he had nothing to learn about how to make Danny feel loved and secure. Danny still needed Dana, but he turned more and more often to Gabe.

The very best times of all were the evenings. Gabe came home early, helped her fix dinner and clean up, played with Danny and helped her put him to bed. Even though things tended to get rather tense after that—they had difficulty being alone in the same room together. Dana cherished the time they had alone, but she didn't dare let him touch her for fear she wouldn't be able to control herself. Even though she liked him more and more each day, even though she shamelessly lusted after his body, she didn't love him. She couldn't let herself.

He still wasn't able to see the real Dana. Until he did see her, she couldn't trust him with her feelings. She had made up her mind she would never marry a man who, like her father, equated her value with her material success.

Yet it would be nice to know he liked her.

"Gabe said you had learned to make dinner all by yourself," Salome said. "I told him he was crazy, that it was just a bridegroom talking."

Dana came back to the world with a start. She'd missed half of what Salome said, but apparently it didn't matter.

"Salome, for goodness sakes, leave her alone," Liz said. "She's got a new husband, a new town, and a new son. She's got more than enough without you hassling her."

"I'm not hassling her," Salome insisted. "If she learns, then I have to learn. And you know how I *hate* anything to do with cooking."

"You don't have to break out the recipe book yet," Dana said, feeling more in sympathy with Salome than ever before. "Gabe is still a much better cook than I am."

"That's what I need," Salome said, "a man who can cook. But you can't find one in this valley. They're brought up expecting to be waited on hand and foot."

"Matt doesn't," Liz said.

"You imported him," Salome pointed out.

Dana was an import, but she didn't mind learning to cook. Once they discovered she genuinely appreciated their help, most women in town couldn't wait to help. She had gotten enough food—with instructions on how to prepare more when that disappeared—than they could eat in the next two weeks.

"Are you deaf, or do I have to ask you a third time?"

"What?" Dana said. "I'm afraid I didn't hear you."

"She's been asking questions that are none of her business," Liz said. "It serves her right to have you ignore her."

"She didn't even hear me," Salome said. "I'll bet she's thinking about what's going to happen tonight after she puts Danny to bed."

"Salome Halfacre, I'm ashamed of you," Liz Dennis said. "That's none of your business."

"Have a heart," Salome said. "You're both married to hunks. All I can do is dream."

Unfortunately that was all Dana could do, too. Or was it?

Chapter Fourteen

Gabe found himself whistling as he hurried home from the shop. The last two weeks had been the best of his life. After the scene at the airport, they'd decided that people ought to see them showing affection. So they kissed when he left in the morning and when he returned in the evening. They kissed when she and Danny came to eat lunch with him, and they kissed when they left. They held hands in church and when they were out with other people. They even shared jokes. Occasionally their eyes would meet and they'd smile, each knowing what the other thought.

Only one thing marred the tranquility of the two weeks. He went through hell keeping his hands off Dana when they were by themselves. He couldn't even kiss her before they went to bed. The one time he'd tried it, Dana had stammered something about carrying their pretense too far and disappeared into her room.

No, into *his* room. And he couldn't think of her sleeping in his bed without becoming rigid with stifled desire. Even though they went to bed earlier than ever—he thought Dana did this so she wouldn't have to spend so much time alone with him—he didn't get enough sleep. He would wake up dreaming of making love to Dana, his body so rigid the pain alone kept him awake. It seemed the more affection she showed toward him in public, the more uneasy she became in private. She managed to appear calm until Danny went to bed. After that she turned as jumpy as a cat on a hot tin roof.

Gabe hadn't managed to stay very calm, either. He reminded himself on an hourly basis that their marriage was only an arrangement, that Dana wanted a career and her freedom, not marriage and a life in a small town. He kept telling himself that he wanted things that way, but if so, why had he gotten to the point his happiness required that she be present.

He would have to talk to her, explain the difficulty he had keeping his hands off her. It sounded awfully crass when he said it that way, but if they had to be together for several more weeks, why couldn't they enjoy each other? They were both mature adults. They could handle it.

He'd talk to her tonight.

Danny and Elton were in the backyard when he reached the house.

"Gabe!" Danny called and came running to him. Gabe picked him up and tossed him in the air. Danny laughed and wanted to be tossed higher.

"Mama says you're not supposed to toss little kids in the air," Elton said. "She says it scrambles their brains."

"It won't scramble Danny's brains," Gabe said, tossing Danny once more. "He's so smart, he'll have lots of brains left over."

"That's what my dad says," Elton said. "Mama says she sometimes wonders if I have any brains at all."

"All moms say that."

"Did your mom say it about you?"

"Still does."

"Did your pa toss you?"

"All the time."

Elton broke into a big grin. "Then it has to be a fudge. Mama says you must be a genius to get Dana to marry you so quick."

"I had to work fast before she went back to New York," Gabe replied, hoping he didn't show his shock at hearing what other people must be saying.

"Pa says it's going to take ankle irons to keep a gal like her in Iron Springs. Is Dana still a gal?"

"Only to an old codger like your pa. Now you'd better head home before your ma calls you for supper."

"We're having liver and onions. I'll wait."

Gabe laughed. "You want to eat supper with us?"

"Naw. I don't mind liver. I just say it 'cause it makes my sister mad. Ma's making her learn how to cook."

Gabe laughed again. "That sounds like me and my sister. We were always on each other about something."

Bittersweet memories. He still couldn't think of losing Mattie without pain.

"Come on, scamp," he said to Danny. "We'd better help Dana start dinner. My stomach's already growling. Give Elton back his ambulance." Danny loved it. When he rolled it across the ground, the light flashed and the siren blared.

"He can keep it," Elton said. "Dad says I'm getting

too big to play with toys. He's going to get me a go-cart.'' Elton walked away whistling through his teeth.

Dana had the portable phone to her ear when Gabe walked into the kitchen.

''I've told you a hundred times why it can't be annulled,'' she said into the phone. ''There's no use going over it again.''

Her parents had called every day since she got back from New York. Her mother called from Switzerland, her father from Bangkok or Singapore or Hong Kong.

Dana held the phone between her head and shoulder while she turned pork chops. He took the fork and finished the pork chops himself. Dana mouthed the word ''thanks'' and rolled her eyes to go along with her look of impatience.

''You'll just have to wait,'' Dana said. ''Nothing you say will change my mind.''

Her father had offered to buy her a partnership in a well-known French antique firm. From what Dana said, Gabe guessed that would have set the old man back at least a million bucks.

''Then stay with father in Tokyo, or wherever he'll be next week. I've got to go, Mother. I'm cooking dinner. It'll burn.''

Their frantic efforts to end their daughter's marriage had angered Gabe at first. Now they just amused him.

''Then don't tell them I cook. Now I really have to go. Bye.''

Dana put the phone down on the counter with uncustomary force. ''Can you have an unlisted number?''

''They'd just call some old crony and get the new one.''

''Maybe I'll disconnect it.''

"Then Ma would be over here every half hour making sure we're all right."

"There's got to be some way to keep my parents from calling. They're about to drive me nuts."

"It won't last forever."

He waited, hoping she'd say something that showed she didn't want it to end. But he knew that wouldn't happen. And in all fairness to Dana, he couldn't let it happen. These few weeks had been a pleasant idyll, but it had to come to an end. Dana constantly talked about what she would do when she went back to work. She looked at him like he ought to be interested. He would smile and pretend to listen, then think about something else. He couldn't let himself brood on how different things would be when she left, so he concentrated on what he and Danny would do together.

Though he liked Dana more and more each day, he didn't want to fall in love with her. It made him too vulnerable. He'd been down that road once, and he still bore the scars. He could still remember how happy he felt the day he and Ellen exchanged vows. He also remembered his plans for the shop, for children, for growing old together in Iron Springs. He remembered even more clearly the pain when Ellen told him what she had done, when she walked out on him.

He and Danny were both alone, perfect for each other. He didn't need love. But if he ever did allow himself to fall in love again, he'd make certain he and his wife were so perfectly matched there couldn't be any possibility of their ever falling out of love. Of all the women he knew, Dana was the one least able to fit that requirement.

No, they would continue their pretense until he got custody. After that—

"Damn! I'll never get dinner ready if this phone keeps ringing," Dana said.

"What do you have left to do?" he asked.

"Just the bread and the salad."

"No problem. Answer the phone."

It was her partner. Dana took the portable phone and went into the den. Gabe never liked it when Sheila called. Dana's career threatened him in a way nothing else could. When Dana didn't come back right away, he knew there was trouble.

"You ready to eat?" he asked Danny.

An unnecessary question. Danny held up his arms to be lifted into his chair. He cut up Danny's pork chop. "Here, scamp. You go ahead. I'll wait for Dana."

The food had gone cold before Dana returned.

"I've got to go to New York," she said. "There's trouble over the authenticity of a piece we sold to a very important client. Sheila falls to pieces over this sort of thing. Really, *really* rich people scare her to death."

"How long will you be gone?"

"A couple of days. Maybe three."

"We'll miss you."

"Lucius's lawyer is going to start sniffing at the trail again."

"You take care of your business. We'll let Marshall worry about Lucius."

"I hate to leave Danny again so soon."

"He knows Naomi and the kids so well he won't mind."

"I know, but—"

"I'll take him over to Ma's every night so he can get his ration of female spoiling. She'll be so happy she'll probably start trouble in New York so you'll have to go up more often. She's been hinting we ought to go away on a honeymoon so she can have him to herself.''

"That's it!'' Dana exclaimed.

"What's it?''

"You can come with me. Lucius can think we're going on our honeymoon.''

"But we won't be.''

"Bring pictures of your best pieces,'' Dana said, ignoring his objections. "I've got several people I want to see them. You'll soon be getting offers that'll make that Middleburg buyer's eyes pop.''

"Dana, I can't just up and leave.''

"Why not? Sam and Billy can take care of the shop for a few days. You just said Naomi and your mother can take care of Danny between them. Do you have a really good camera? We can wait until we get to New York to get the photos developed.''

Gabe had no earthly reason to go to New York. He didn't even like the place. He wouldn't have anything to do while Dana took care of her business, and he didn't really care if no one ever paid top price for his furniture.

But he caught Dana's excitement. Before he knew it, he had entered into her plans, adding his own suggestions. All the while, he kept telling himself to stay home, that this would make things harder in the end. But he'd be lying if he pretended he wouldn't jump at the chance to spend several days with Dana. He'd been trying to think of an excuse to do just that. Now that the perfect opportunity had been dropped in his lap, he couldn't turn it down.

"Confess, New York isn't as bad as you thought it would be,'' Dana said. She and Gabe were in a taxi heading toward her apartment. She was relaxed and tired after a long day and a leisurely dinner. She hardly noticed the noise.

"I still wouldn't want to live here."

"I wasn't talking about that."

"Okay, it's not so bad."

Dana laughed. "Hurt yourself. Give it a little praise. After all the compliments you've had on your furniture, you ought to be walking on air."

"I'll wait until I see the color of their money before I get excited," Gabe said.

They had taken an early-morning flight. Dana had gotten her business straightened out in a matter of two hours, and they had spent the afternoon showing Gabe's photographs. New York buyers were pretty cagey, but several asked to see more of his work. Sheila had been enthusiastic about putting several pieces in their showroom. Gabe hadn't said yes to any of this yet, but she intended to give him all the time he needed.

Dana couldn't make the decision for him. Putting himself at the mercy of the international market with its ability to make or break a reputation required a thick hide. She had no doubt he'd succeed, but he had to want it enough to take the chance. Gabe gave the impression of being unmoved by other people's opinions. But she knew something of creative artists and their fragile egos. She wondered if part of Gabe's reason for staying in Iron Springs wasn't a reluctance to expose his work to the evaluation of strangers who valued a piece of furniture more by its commercial value than the artistry that went into its making. A little bit of Gabe went into everything he made. That little piece was safe in Iron Springs.

Within a couple of hours after the plane landed, Dana knew bringing Gabe to New York had been the smartest decision she'd ever made. During the most difficult part of the negotiations she only had to look up, see Gabe, and know a huge slice of her life didn't depend on whether a deal fell through, if a customer was unhappy. Most important of all, she didn't have to depend on it for her own fulfillment. She liked her work, and she didn't intend to turn her back on it, but other things were more important.

She knew that now because she loved Gabe. Not the way she had when she was a teenager. She had been in love with a fantasy, had thought only of what she wanted and needed, not what she had to give. Looking back on it now, she wondered why she hadn't forgotten him long ago. If she hadn't been best friends with Mattie, she might have.

She still thought of what she wanted from Gabe, but she thought, too, of the many things she wanted to do for him. She wanted to give him the confidence to face the New York critics, to help guide him through the shoals of the New York market. She wanted to help restore some of his faith in women. He liked them, lusted after them, but he didn't trust them with his heart. She wanted to give him the family he so desperately wanted, help turn his big house into the home he'd envisioned when he bought it.

She'd dated enough men to know Gabe was one in a million. His being mind-numbingly handsome didn't hurt. She didn't mind his being so big and strong she felt warm and protected. Neither did she mind that he seemed to find her just as attractive.

He took his duties and obligations seriously. He'd committed himself to becoming a good guardian for Danny. He'd not only learned to play with Danny, he devoted all his free time to helping the child learn to love him. He'd actually cut back on the time he spent at the shop. She knew how much Gabe's work meant to him, what a sacrifice that represented.

She liked his commitment to his family and community. She'd never felt as if she belonged anywhere, had never felt part of anything. Maybe that's why she'd held so tightly to Mattie's friendship.

Buried deep inside her, almost out of sight, even to herself, had been a desperate desire to be needed and loved. She had denied its existence when she could, said it didn't matter when she couldn't, done with substitutes when she couldn't find anything else. Her grandmother had been a substitute for her parents, Mattie and Danny a substitute for the family she didn't have, her work a means of putting a value on a life no one else seemed able to appreciate.

Over the past weeks she'd come to see that she and Gabe were very much like lighthouses helping guide other lives to safety only to be left in lonely isolation when they were no longer needed. His father's inability to love had caused a rift in his home. His sister and wife had left him. He didn't trust love. He was reaching out to Danny, holding on to the child in hopes that a child's innocent love could fill the need.

Dana knew it wouldn't.

She'd finally been able to pick out the really important things in life, the things that could give her true happiness. She could reach out for what she wanted despite being afraid. Gabe still couldn't. If only he could learn to trust her, they could each find the happiness that had eluded them so far.

"How can you live in a place like this?" Gabe finally asked.

"You get used to it," she said.

"How do you sleep?"

She laughed. "I used to ask my grandmother that when the rooster woke me first thing in the morning on the farm."

"You are comparing a rooster to this!" he asked when they got out of the cab.

The noise hit her like a fist. Two cab drivers seemed to be trying to settle an altercation with their horns. A garbage truck was backing up, a jackhammer pounding into concrete somewhere. She didn't remember it being so loud.

"It's quieter in the apartment," she said.

She paid for the cab. Gabe carried their luggage inside. The double doors to the apartment building acted like a sound barrier. She could hardly hear the noise from the street.

"I wouldn't have believed it," Gabe said.

"We do manage to get a few things right," she said.

"I'm not convinced yet."

The moment they stepped into her apartment, the mood changed.

"You have a nice place," Gabe said.

"It's easy to have a nice place when you're in the antique business. You just furnish it with the pieces nobody else wants."

"These don't look like rejects."

"Of course, you need a few really good pieces."

"Then you have a genius for melding the genuine with the not-so-good."

"Next time Sheila comes in, I'll have you talk to her," Dana said. "She always questions my judgment."

Yet despite the friendly banter, tension continued to build until Gabe set his suitcase down.

"I shouldn't have come here," he said. "I should have taken a room in a hotel."

"Don't be ridiculous. Lucius's lawyer would be on us in a minute. I've got three bedrooms."

"It would be a mistake if you had a hundred bedrooms."

She knew what he meant. She had felt the same tension every night after they put Danny to bed. She practically had to lock herself in her bedroom to keep from throwing herself at him.

"I'm going to change into something more comfortable. Fix yourself a drink. There's whisky in the cabinet, and the wine rack is full."

She picked up her suitcase and fled.

Postponing it only prolonged the tension between them, Dana realized. They'd been sitting apart all evening, she on one sofa, Gabe on the other. They acted like two strangers nervous at being left in each other's company. Not even two glasses of wine eased the tension.

"Are we going to keep talking around it?" Gabe asked.

"Talking around what?" She knew, but she couldn't bring herself to admit it.

"That I want to go to bed with you," Gabe stated bluntly. "That I don't know if I can stay in this apartment if we don't."

"I don't want you to leave." Why must she act like a featherbrain? Why didn't she have the guts to say what she felt. "I want that, too," she managed to say. Her voice sounded unlike itself. She felt her body tremble, but she didn't lower her gaze. She looked right into

Gabe's eyes. "I've been thinking about it for some time now."

Air escaped Gabe as from a punctured tube. "Why didn't you say so? I've been practically killing myself to keep from touching you."

She couldn't tell him she had fallen in love with him. He still thought of her as some kind of exotic life form. She didn't want to scare him away.

"I may be a modern woman, but I'm still traditional enough to want the man to make the first move."

He made the move almost before the words were out of her mouth. He crossed the distance that separated them, sat next to her on the couch, dropped his hands on her shoulders. "You don't know what an agony it's been to keep away from you."

"A woman always likes to hear she's practically irresistible."

"Men must say that to you all the time."

"Rather often. Only I've noticed they had a problem with commitment." She had begun to wonder if there was something wrong with her, something she and other women couldn't see but something men would notice immediately.

"They must be fools."

"You're not a fool."

"Yes, I am. If I weren't, you wouldn't have to tell me any of this."

She wanted to know how he could expect himself to be sensitive to the hidden feelings of a woman he didn't love. What he wanted centered on lust and desire. Things that had little to do with her feeling for him.

Or had lust drawn her into his arms? Maybe a little bit. The need to be held by the man she loved? That, too. But just as strong was the need to reach out to Gabe, to convince him not every woman was unworthy of trust, of his love. Maybe she could be the one to convince him he still could have the home and family he wanted so badly. She leaned forward and kissed him lightly on the lips.

"Now we both know, so we don't have to worry about it any longer."

Their lips met in a series of sweet, puckered kisses. "Who's worried?"

She worried he would think his attraction for her was only physical. She thought he liked her a lot. His feelings might even be a good deal stronger than that, but he couldn't admit it.

"I've dreamed of this almost from the moment you walked into Marshall's kitchen," he said as he kissed the side of her mouth, along the line of her jaw.

"Do you always want to go to bed with women you don't like?" she managed to ask, despite the currents that flew around her body making her muscles unsteady and undependable.

"I didn't know you very well."

"What do you think of me now?"

He took her face in his hands and held it gently. "That you're completely different from what I thought."

"Do you like the difference?"

"What do you think?"

He pulled her roughly, almost violently, to him. The hunger of his kisses shattered any lingering doubt that he wanted her as badly as she wanted him. But she cautioned herself not to read too much into his eagerness. She reminded herself a man could be driven by a physical need that had nothing to do with his emotions, that the intensity of his actions didn't translate directly into love. She tried to tell herself that just because she loved Gabe didn't mean he loved her in return.

But she wanted to feel that he loved her, that he was showing her what he couldn't say, what he was *afraid* to put into words.

No woman could reason clearly when the man she loved held her in a tight embrace and covered her with hot, hungry kisses. She could only think she wanted him to kiss her, wanted him to hold her so tightly her bones protested, wanted to feel she dominated his thoughts to the point of obsession, that desire to possess her burned though his veins like fire consuming a long fuse, coming closer and closer to the emotional dynamite they both tried to keep under control.

His hands moved up and down her body, tracing the ridge of her spine, splayed against the expanse of her back, cupping the curve of her shoulders, each movement pressing her body more tightly against his, causing her skin to tingle and become sensitive to his touch. She arched against him, needing to feel imprisoned in his arms.

Gabe kissed the side of her neck, her throat. She felt his fingers on her blouse, undoing the buttons. His touch penetrated the fabric, her satin slip, her bra, and reached her breasts, causing tiny prickles to dance over her skin. Dana's breaths became deeper, taken-in gulps rather than a calm flow. When his hands moved across her breasts, her heart thudded, then sped to a stronger, faster rhythm.

Reaching inside her blouse, he cupped her breast in his large hand. Dana gasped and pressed her body against him, hoping to intensify the feeling that had slowly begun to spread to the rest of her body. Gabe pulled her blouse loose from her skirt and slipped it off her shoulders. He then covered her shoulders, collarbone and the tops of her breasts with hot kisses, while his hand gently stroked her flesh, rubbing her nipple until it strained against the material of her bra.

Dana let herself fall back until she lay flat on the sofa. As Gabe moved to readjust his position, she was scorched by the heat of his gaze. She saw vulnerability, too. She had seen it before, but never so clearly. He might not be able to say it—he might not even *want* to say it—but at this moment he needed her as much as she needed him. Never had she felt so wanted, so needed, by anyone.

It made her even more determined to convince Gabe each of them was the answer to the other's happiness.

Gabe's hand managed to undo the clasp to her bra, but couldn't manage the tangle of straps.

"Let's move to the bedroom," she said. He looked reluctant, as if he were afraid movement would break the spell. "It'll be easier."

Disentangling themselves and getting up was awkward. It did destroy some of the heat that had built up between them, but Dana didn't intend to give their mood time to cool. She stepped out of her skirt and headed for the bedroom, removing the rest of her clothes as she went. Gabe followed suit. When he joined her on the bed moments later, they were both naked.

His first touch on her breast caused her to jump.

Gabe pulled his hand back.

She took his hand and placed it on her breast. It felt icy cold against her hot skin. She welcomed the contrast. It sent an extra volley of sensations rocketing through her. She'd almost forgotten what a man's touch could do to her body. Not that anyone's touch could compare to Gabe's.

When he moved closer, kissed her nipples with his

hot lips, she knew Gabe would always be unique for her. No other man had had the power to lift her off the bed simply by touching her body. She moved closer to him, anxious for more of his touch, for more of the heat that flowed from him in a rushing torrent.

She stopped when she felt his arousal against her.

"Don't be afraid," he said.

"I'm not." She needed more of Gabe, more of his assurances that she meant more to him than a momentary physical release. She took his face in her hands, pulled his lips to hers. "Hold me," she said.

He moved even closer, wrapped his arms around her. When she felt him prodding against her even more insistently, she didn't pull away. Wrapped in his embrace, she felt needed, wanted and loved.

She'd always known Gabe was a big man, but she didn't realize how big until she couldn't get her arms around him. It made her feel small, and she liked that. Being described as tall and statuesque had never sounded as appealing to her as petite and dainty. *Independent* and *self-assured* also lacked warmth. For a change she wanted to feel vulnerable, cared for, protected.

She had been held by several men, but none had been able to give her the same sense of completeness as feeling Gabe's arms around her, his breath warm against her cheek, his body shielding hers. She'd spent years looking for where she belonged.

Now she'd found it, and she didn't mean to let go.

Gabe claimed her mouth once again as his hands moved beween them to cup her breasts. Their breaths rose in crescendo together, their heartbeats accelerated in unison. Her breasts started to ache from his touch, to send tiny electric charges all over her body. But even as he took her nipple in his hot mouth, she became aware of the fire that had begun to build in her belly. Gabe's lips made her nipples pebble-hard, generating waves of desire that eddied out from her belly like ripples on a pond.

The ripples grew bigger and closer together when Gabe's hand moved down to cup her bottom, to pull her hard against him. Acting on impulse, she reached between them, took him in her grasp.

"Careful." The word came from Gabe on a shuddered breath.

"I didn't mean to hurt you."

"You didn't. It's just that men are more explosive than women."

His moving her hand to his back disappointed her, but that vanished when she moved it across to his rear end. She'd always thought Gabe had a spectacular behind. Now she knew it. She moved her hand up the broad expanse of his back, felt the muscles moving smoothly underneath his skin—that excited her in a way merely touching him hadn't. There was something sensual about the feel of muscles, something sexual about their fluid movement. She'd never noticed that before. But then she'd never been in the arms of a man as strong as Gabe.

The feeling of his hand drew her attention abruptly as it moved between her thighs. She'd been so engrossed in her own explorations, she had missed its journey from her breast, across her belly to the inside of her thigh. But she didn't miss anything when Gabe parted her flesh, and slowly began to enter her. She felt her muscles clamp down. Through a conscious effort she relaxed, opened to him. She didn't feel afraid, shocked or surprised. She didn't understand why everything Gabe did felt as though it was happening to her for the first time.

Gabe had found her tiny nub of intense feeling, and the heat in her belly changed to a flame. Waves of fire pulsed from her center, gathering all of her into its heat. Gabe continued to tease the nub, rub it, until tiny waves of pleasure rolled through her. Small at first, they quickly escalated in intensity until she felt consumed by them. Her realization that the moaning sounds were coming from her only served to heighten her awareness that what was happening between them had moved far beyond her experience or her ability to control it.

She heard herself gasping, felt her body lunging with aching desire. The more she wanted the agony to stop, the more she wanted it to increase. The more she cried out against what Gabe was doing, the more she wanted him to continue.

Then suddenly the waves crested and spilled over, the pulsing slowed, and the tension drained from her like hot liquid, leaving her throbbing and open.

But even as she felt her muscles release their iron grip on her bones, felt her body relax into the mattress, felt the fire in her veins recede toward its source, Gabe moved to cover her body, to enter her fully. The waves of fire and pleasure rose again.

She wrapped her body around him, trying to draw him deep enough inside her to reach the need that had never been touched. The fire spread again, hotter than ever, but still she couldn't quite fill the deep emptiness. She rose to meet Gabe, matching him thrust for thrust, panting breath for panting breath, striving to burn away the remorseless need that wouldn't let her rest.

Their lovemaking was frenzied, their slick bodies wrapped so tightly together, she felt melded to Gabe, that they had become one entity, bound together forever. In opening herself to him, trusting him, she felt free of all restraint, all bonds. The waves tossed her higher and higher until she was certain she could never come down to earth again, that she'd die of disappointment if she did.

She was reaching, reaching, almost touching. And just as she did, the waves broke over her, and everything subsided beneath her. Gently she floated back to earth, her body drained, that little corner of her soul no longer empty.

Chapter Fifteen

Dana smiled to herself as they lay in the bed side by side, silent except for the sound of their rapid breathing. Gabe had continued to make passionate love to her every night since they returned from New York. Everything they said or did stirred some memory of their two days and nights in New York.

Their lovemaking had gotten better each time, but tonight there had been greater intensity, more depth, more sense of sharing. Maybe that came from being back home. Maybe it came from accepting her feelings for Gabe. But Dana didn't know what Gabe's feelings were. She'd never told him how she felt for fear he wouldn't feel the same way. It scared her to death that it might be impossible for him to love her as much as she loved him. At the same time it seemed equally impossible that, loving him as much as she did, he couldn't love her and want them to be together for the rest of their lives.

But he hadn't talked about his feelings for her or the future. From her experience of men, nothing frightened them more than commitment, especially a commitment that would last the rest of their lives. Gabe had been badly burned once. It wouldn't be easy for him to put himself at risk again.

But she had to know. Even if knowing would break her heart. She told herself she couldn't wait any longer, but even thinking of the words, forming them on her lips seemed impossible.

In the end the words she spoke were the precise words she had made up her mind not to say. "I love you."

The sound of the words shocked and frightened her. They sounded so different, so powerful, so life altering, she wondered if she could really mean them.

Gabe didn't respond.

"I said I love you."

She said it with more confidence this time. Her feelings wouldn't change even if he couldn't love her in return.

"I heard," Gabe said.

He didn't sound like a man who'd been told something he wanted to hear. She reached out, put her hand on his shoulder. He didn't move, but she felt him stiffen. She took her hand away.

"I've been wanting to tell you, even before we went to New York," she said, "but I was afraid you'd act like this."

"I'm not acting like anything," Gabe said. "I'm just surprised."

"You're more than surprised. You're shocked."

"Okay, I'm shocked. We're completely different. We don't want the same things. You're committed to your career, your life in New York. There's nothing in Iron Springs that could make you want to live here.''

''You. Danny.''

He didn't respond, but she was certain he didn't believe her. ''My priorities and commitments have changed. I know this seems sudden, but it isn't. Not really. Everything started to change when Mattie moved in. It changed even more when Danny was born. I didn't realize it at the time because I was too busy to pay attention to my feelings. Lots of things changed without my realizing it.'' Why didn't he say something? The silence frightened her. ''After your father's and Mattie's death and finding yourself Danny's guardian, you probably felt a little like that.''

''Feeling sad, hurt and overwhelmed isn't the same. I haven't changed my feelings about anything important. I've only added Danny to my family.''

A numbing cold crept through Dana's limbs. She shivered and sat up. She guessed she had her answer.

''We've only been playacting for the benefit of the judge and Lucius's lawyer.'' Gabe sounded as though he was trying to convince himself. ''You've been talking nearly every day about what you want to do when you get back to New York.''

How odd that people could so misunderstand each other. ''I was trying to convince myself I really wanted to go back to New York. But I hoped you'd ask me to stay.''

''Would you?''

''What we have together is what's important, not where we live.''

''Where I live is important to me. I can't fulfill my obligations anywhere else.''

"Don't you have an obligation to yourself to be happy?"

"As soon as I get custody of Danny, I'll be happy."

She wanted to reach over and touch him, kiss him, put her hands all over him until he couldn't keep himself from taking her into his arms. But she had some few shreds of pride.

She had no idea how she could convince Gabe they ought to stay married, but she knew he loved her. She couldn't believe he could make love to her the way he had without feeling something akin to love. Besides, she knew how he looked at her when he thought she wasn't looking. She knew naked hunger when she saw it. She also knew loneliness, longing for something out of reach.

"I won't pretend I'm not attracted to you," Gabe said. His voice sounded under tight control. "I can't be in the same house with you all the time, sleep in the room next to you, and keep my hands off of you. If it upsets you, I'll sleep at my mother's house."

"That would be all that's needed to convince the judge to hand Danny over to Lucius."

"Then you can move Danny's bed in here."

"Gabe, I don't need protection. I like making love to you. I want to do it again and again. I'm saying that I love you, that I think you love me, that we can be the family Danny needs, the kind of family we both want."

"What about your career?" he asked. "And let's not forget your parents. They'd move heaven and earth to keep you from marrying me or living in Iron Springs."

"I'm not going to marry to please my parents. I don't know what I want to do about my career just now, but we can work something out."

"What if you can't? What if you decide you hate Iron Springs and never want to come back here again."

"I won't."

"Your mother did. Even my wife did, and she grew up in the valley."

"I'm not Ellen."

"No. You've got even less reason to want to live here."

"We don't have to live here, not all the time. And I don't mean you have to desert your business or your friends. New York would be the perfect place for you. You could get three or four times as much for your work. You could develop a bigger shop, make more furniture, make more money."

"I'm not interested in a bigger shop or more money. I make furniture because I enjoy doing the work myself. It wouldn't be the same if I had a whole roomful of assistants."

"You have Sam and Billy."

"We're partners. We do everything together. They're like family."

"You could take them to New York."

"They'd be as out of place as I would be."

"You could be comfortable anywhere you wanted to be. Try it for six months, even a month—"

Gabe heaved himself up in the bed so suddenly he caused Dana to cut off her sentence.

"There's no point in talking about this," he said. "It just makes things harder. We ought to go ahead with things the way we planned."

"Have you thought about what a divorce would do to Danny?"

"We knew from the first we'd be getting divorced," he said.

"What if Lucius brings the case up again?"

Gabe got up from the bed and reached for his clothes.

"I'll figure out something else, but I don't think we ought to stay married."

He left the room, taking with him all the warmth and her happiness.

Gabe had been miserable all week. He couldn't pretend otherwise. Neither could he deny Dana was the problem, because he was falling in love with Dana. He could feel it happening minute by minute. He didn't need to be alone with her to be forcefully reminded of how much he liked being with her, how much he needed her. That would seal his fate all the more quickly.

He couldn't allow himself to love her. It would never work.

He'd finally realized it wasn't about New York. He didn't like big cities of any kind. He knew choosing to live in a remote mountain village had been an expensive choice, but he didn't regret it. He knew what he'd given up—at least he thought he did—and he willingly paid the price.

It wasn't about her career. He didn't have any objection to the woman he wanted to marry having a career, as long as that didn't exclude children and a close relationship with him.

He accepted the evidence of his own eyes and admitted Dana had changed. She would never be the stay-at-home wife he'd envisioned when he married Ellen, but she did want a family, she did like living in Iron Springs.

He just didn't believe she'd changed enough for him to trust his heart again.

There, he'd finally said it. He was afraid to fall in love. Big, strong, confident Gabe Purvis trembled in fear of a little old emotion that could take a man like him and turn him inside out, leave him helpless.

Wasn't he helpless already? He hadn't been this miserable in years. He couldn't stay away from Dana when then were together. No matter what he vowed during the day, his resolve evaporated the minute he stepped in the house and she smiled at him. He called himself a liar, a cheat, a fraud, but it made no difference. The moment they put Danny to bed, he would make hot, passionate love to Dana, sometimes not letting her fall asleep until midnight. He would wake up renewed, invigorated, only to beat himself down during the day because he had no willpower. He would go home determined that *this* time things would be different.

Then he would do it all over again.

Because the way he looked at Dana had changed. All the things he used to think were so important to her— the things that stood between them—had disappeared. He no longer thought of her as a woman obsessed with career, success or independence. Just a woman looking for love, generous, able to give more love than she got.

Now he could respect her decisions, admire some of them. *And that despite disagreeing with her half the time!* No wonder he felt as if he was going in circles.

The most unexpected thing she'd done was create a life for the three of them that he'd come to depend on. He loved breakfast and dinner. They cooked together, ate together, cleaned up together. And he looked forward to lunch when she and Danny would come to the shop. Dana would sit quietly, smiling while Danny bubbled over with things he'd done at day care.

Gabe especially liked the time after dinner. He and Danny would play on the floor while Dana watched. Lately they'd been able to talk her into joining them. He'd never realized how much fun she could be.

Then there was their time together after Danny had

gone to sleep. His body began to swell just thinking about it.

She had set her trap and baited it with just about everything he'd ever wanted. And like an unsuspecting fool, he'd walked straight into it. Now he didn't know if he could stand to be set free.

But he would be. The judge would make his decision in a couple of weeks. If he didn't agree to stay married to Dana, she would go back to New York.

But could he trust any woman to want the same things he wanted when even his sister had been willing to do almost anything to get away from that very life-style?

No. He'd had one disastrous marriage because he'd misjudged a woman, and it had nearly destroyed him. It had made him unaware of what was happening to his own sister. It had kept him from supporting his mother when she might have been able to prevent the rift in his family. His own confusion had kept him from confronting his father's stubborn refusal to accept Mattie's right to independence.

No. It was too dangerous. He could learn to love Dana in a way that had never been possible with Ellen. If Ellen's leaving had torn him apart, what would Dana's walking out on him do?

It would destroy him. No, he couldn't risk it. He had to think of Danny.

But thinking of Danny brought him back to Dana. No woman could love Danny more than she did. This very same love had brought about the change in her, caused her to create a warm home environment for Danny, an environment in which she wanted to include Gabe. All he had to do was accept what he'd been given.

But to do that would mean trusting his heart again, and he couldn't do that.

So the argument went round and round in his head until he greeted his mother's arrival at his workshop with relief. "What are you doing here?" he asked. She never came to the shop. She said the smell of the paints and chemicals gave her a headache.

"I want to know what's bothering you."

His mother never beat around the bush. If she wanted something, she asked flat-out.

"Nothing's wrong. I've just been working extra hard to make up for the time I spent in New York."

"I didn't come here to listen to the fibs you tell yourself. Or any you're telling Dana. I want to know the truth."

That was the problem with mothers. They could always tell when you weren't telling the truth. Even when you were telling half-truths.

"What makes you think something's wrong?"

Being evasive never worked, but he wanted to know if everybody else in Iron Springs could see him tearing himself apart.

"You're acting just like your father when he had something in his craw. He wouldn't say a word, just walked around looking as if he'd bite you in half if you dared speak to him. When you start doing that to Billy and Sam, boys you've known all your life, something's wrong."

"Nothing I can't handle."

"Then there's Dana."

"What about Dana?" Dana had gotten to be good friends with Liz and Salome, but he didn't believe she would have said anything to his mother.

"Dana's walking around looking like she's frozen stiff," his mother said. "She laughs and smiles, tries to give the impression she's happy when it's perfectly obvious she's miserable. The only person who could make her that miserable is you. I want to know what you've done to her.''

Just what he needed, his mother to take Dana's side. "I haven't done anything.''

"Then what haven't you done that you should have done?''

"Why do you think if there's anything wrong it has to be my fault?''

"Most women learn early on they have to compromise, to bend. Men come up thinking they can have everything their own way. When they don't get it, they make everybody miserable. Now, what's going on?''

He resented being put in the wrong. He just wanted to raise Danny, to give the kid as much love and family support as he could. Good intentions, but they'd gotten him caught between what he wanted to do and what he felt he ought to do. Either way he turned he'd be miserable.

He hadn't intended to tell his mother why he and Dana got married, but he had tired of hiding behind a lie. It had made Dana and him miserable. Best to get it out in the open.

"Sit down," he said, using a cloth to brush the dust off an old folding chair. "I've got something to tell you, and you're not going to like it.''

He told her everything, especially the fact that he thought he was falling in love with her.

He had to give his mother credit. She didn't faint, turn red in the face, or tell him he was a fool. She just listened.

"You're playing a mighty dangerous game," she said when she finished.

"I know.''

"I'm not sure I'd have done the same thing, but given how things have turned out, I don't see why you're so upset. It looks to me like you've fallen in whipped cream despite doing your best to land in the ditch."

"What could a woman like Dana and me have in common?"

"Do you love her?"

"I don't know."

"I think you do."

"Well I'm still not sure." It irritated him that every woman thought she could tell him what he was feeling when he didn't know himself.

"If you don't love her, it won't make any difference how much you have in common," his mother said. "And if you do, you'll find the things you have in common are a lot more important that the things you don't."

"Is that the way it was with you and Dad?"

That question stopped her. Maybe it was unfair, but he had to ask it.

"Yes, except for not letting Mattie go to college. I made a mistake there. I think I could have brought him around if I'd tried, but I was afraid."

"Of what?"

"Losing him."

"Dad would never have divorced you."

"If I'd lost your Dad, divorce would have been easier than living with him."

"I don't understand."

"Then you don't love Dana the way you ought."

"What do you mean by that?"

"You're still afraid of loving her. If you *really* loved her, you wouldn't let anything stop you."

"How can you say that after what happened with Ellen?"

"Dana and Ellen have no more in common than Ellen and I do."

"Ma, look at the facts. Outside of Danny, we'd have nothing to keep us together."

He knew that wasn't true the moment he said it. Even before the trip to New York they'd found plenty of shared interests.

His mother stood and brushed nonexistent dust from her dress. "If what I suspect is true, you're letting the best thing that's ever happened to you slip away for the want of a little courage."

"I'm not a coward."

"You never have been except where Dana's concerned. Even when she was a little girl, you used to keep your distance. Now you're letting one mistake make you afraid to trust your heart."

"I'm not afraid. I told—"

"All of us have to take chances to find what we want, son. Sometimes it's only a small chance. Sometimes it's a really big one. If your happiness is at stake, don't you think it's worth taking a chance?"

"It could just as easily be my future misery. If I thought it could work—"

"Maybe you can make it work. No one can guarantee that. You have to have the courage to try. Now I've lectured enough. I told Dana to bring you and Danny over for dinner tonight. I'm making chicken and dumplings, and you can't make that for just one person."

"Ma—"

"Don't be a fool, Gabe. Everything you ever wanted is being handed to you. Don't keep telling me she's different. If you want this marriage, or any marriage, to work, you're going to have to make some compromises."

''There are some things you can compromise on and others you can't.''

''I know. Just make sure you haven't mixed up the *can't*'s with the *can*'s.''

''How do you know which is which?''

''You don't, not always. Some things you take on faith. Other times you take a chance and hope things will work.''

Chapter Sixteen

"She's a genius," Liz Dennis said to Gabe. "You ought to see the list of buyers she's lined up for the fair. New York, Chicago, Philadelphia, even Boston. She's even talked Amos into holding rooms for them in the hotel for that weekend."

Liz had commissioned Gabe to make a desk for Matt. She came in every day to check on his progress and to report on Dana's latest accomplishment. When she exhausted that subject, she would tell him again she didn't know how they survived at the clinic before Dana started to volunteer. Salome had already asked Matt to put her on the payroll.

"We have only local merchandise," Gabe said "What are those buyers going to find to interest them?"

"She talked the committee into letting her invite people from the whole valley. Then she got on the Internet and found names and addresses of people from Pennsylvania to Tennessee who craft handmade products. If they all come, we'll have enough for several fairs.''

Liz wasn't the only person who seemed determined to make certain Gabe knew each one of the miracles Dana worked on behalf of the fair. He would have sworn every person in town had taken a vow to keep him informed on an hourly basis.

''I can see why she made such a success of her antique business,'' Liz said.

''How do you know about that?'' Both of them had been careful to say nothing of the business.

''She wasn't bragging,'' Liz assured him, ''though she would have every reason to if she wanted. She told us she owned part of a business, that she was taking a long vacation on her doctor's advice. I just happened to mention the name to my ex-husband's wife. She couldn't believe I actually knew one of the owners. She said she can't afford to shop there.''

''Dana's clients are rather wealthy.''

''That's what Phyllis said. We're very lucky to have had her help us.''

Others weren't quite so subtle.

''I don't know what you're going to do to keep her in Iron Springs,'' Josie Woodhouse said.

''I'm not going to do anything to keep her here,'' Gabe said from between clenched teeth. ''Dana never intended to give up her career.''

''She can't live here and in New York. She'll have to choose.''

Gabe didn't need Josie to tell him that.

''Will you move to New York with her?'' Josie asked.

''I expect to continue working here.''

''Then you'll never keep her,'' Josie stated. ''You make beautiful furniture, but there nothing exciting about furniture. It's dull. Some slick operator will snap her up right from under your nose. You ought to get her pregnant as soon as you can. Having a baby changes women. If you give her two or three kids, you just might be able to keep her.''

In other words, he wasn't enough man for Dana. He needed children to keep her.

Josie was probably right. He'd dated several women in college. Furniture didn't excite any of them. Ellen had married him—he assumed she had loved him—but it hadn't been enough to make her stick with a man who lived on the edge of nowhere and spent his days cutting trees into little pieces of wood.

How on earth did he think he could hold a woman like Dana?

He couldn't. Only a fool would think he could. What did he have to offer? Nothing but Danny. And he didn't have him yet. He couldn't afford to forget she had married him only to keep Danny from Lucius. Maybe she didn't really love him, just thought she did. She'd never had a normal life, a husband, a child, a home, a community, a place where she felt she belonged. After growing up on that merry-go-round her parents called a life, she just loved being valued and appreciated for herself rather than how many antiques she could sell this week or how much money she made.

People in Iron Springs were more interested in whether Danny had had his two-year-old inoculations, how a new cake recipe turned out, how your husband's lumbago was doing, if your daughter's pregnancy was going well, if your boy was happy working in Texas. People things. Not opening nights, not charity balls attended by hundreds of millionaires. Definitely not apartments in Paris or vacation homes in Switzerland. Nothing Dana was used to.

He forced himself to concentrate on Liz Dennis's desk. She wanted it for Matt's birthday. If he didn't keep his mind on his work, it wouldn't be ready, and Liz would have his hide.

But he couldn't get Dana out of his thoughts. He didn't understand how he could be so infatuated with a woman with whom he had virtually nothing in common. He was acting like a child after a piece of candy. He ought to know better. Experience had taught him a mistake like this would be extremely painful. It would be stupid to let his heart overrule his head. He should be concentrating on Danny. The child would soon be totally dependent on him.

He'd always wanted children. Watching Danny grow up would give him the feeling of love and belonging he missed. He, his mother and Danny. That was all that was left of his family.

Surely he didn't need anything else.

"Everyone says this is the best fair we've ever had," Gabe's mother told him. "It's all Dana's doing."

Gabe had seen very little of Dana during the past week. The phone rang from the moment they got up until they went to bed. It had been so bad one night he'd unplugged it. He'd hardly seen her at all during the past three days.

"I've never seen so many people," Mrs. Purvis said as they walked around the booths. "Marshall said the cars were parked all over the fields and down the road for miles. I don't know where Dana found them all."

He didn't know, either. Apparently she had a magical ability to empty the countryside for miles around.

"Lots of people have come over from Charlottes-ville."

The people from Charlottesville didn't concern Gabe as much as a certain buyer from New York. The man had latched on to Dana the minute he arrived on Friday. He'd introduced himself as an old family friend, much too old to stand on ceremony. He kissed and hugged Dana in a far-more-than-friendly manner. Gabe was about ready to remove him by the shirt collar when Dana pushed him away with a reminder she was a married woman.

Kyle—that was his name, Kyle Estabrook—had laughed and said that was no reason to keep them from having fun. He had promptly staked his claim to Dana as his personal guide. Gabe had been strongly tempted to deliver a hard right to the jaw and put him on a plane back to New York before he regained consciousness. When he muttered just that to Dana, she laughed and said several of the buyers were here at her personal in-vitation. She intended to make sure they enjoyed them-selves enough to want to come back next year. By the time the third buyer fawned over Dana like his own pri-vate property, Gabe had to leave before he embarrassed everybody by punching them all out.

He should have been more concerned about the buyers who came by his shop. In one day he got more offers than he could satisfy in a year. By the end of the second, he had stopped accepting business cards. The amounts of money offered still made his head spin.

Sam and Billy were so excited they could hardly con-tain themselves long enough to talk to the buyers. Sam had already picked out his truck. Billy had made Dana promise to buy him a plane ticket the minute one of their pieces went on display. Both kept pestering Gabe, wanting to know if he had ordered his lathe.

Gabe hadn't given any thought to his lathe. He couldn't stop thinking about Dana, wondering what might be happening behind his back. The fact that Dana managed to keep her friends' behavior within bounds didn't help much. Having other men interested in his wife—and not being able to turn them away because she really *wasn't* his wife—had nearly driven him crazy. His mother, with the help of Elton, had volunteered to take care of Danny for the weekend. She had intended it to leave Gabe free to concentrate on his furniture. Instead it left him free to worry about Dana. Never in his life had he been prey to the demon of jealousy. During the weekend he'd made up for a decade of lost time.

But with the knife edge of jealousy came understanding. He loved Dana. It didn't matter that it wasn't sensible, wasn't rational, that it *was* dangerous. He loved her, anyway. If he didn't do something quickly, he could lose her. He left the house and headed toward the center of town and the fair.

Things usually had thinned out by 3:00 p.m. on Sunday afternoon, but not this year. It took Gabe several minutes to realize Dana was nowhere to be found.

"You looking for Dana?" Josie Woodhouse asked.

"Yes," Gabe replied. "Have you seen her?"

"Sure did. She went off with that Kyle fella, the one that's been hanging around her closer than a necklace ever since he got here." She had a look on her face that pretty much said *I told you so you stupid jackass.*

"He's a friend of the family."

"He wants to *be part of the family.*"

"Since Dana's already married to me, that's impossible."

"Not according to him."

"What do you mean?" Gabe had an uneasy feeling he knew.

"He seems to think your marriage will be over in a couple of weeks."

Dana's parents must have told him about the marriage. That's why he acted as if he owned her. He *knew* Dana would be back in New York anytime now.

"He's a real talkative fella," Josie said.

"His kind usually is."

"He said Dana's doctor is the one who made her stay in Iron Springs. Said she needed to get away from the pressure of business."

He looked at the crowd, the hundreds of new buyers and sellers. The fair was at least three times as big as ever before. Dana couldn't help but do things in a big way, even when she was on vacation.

"He said he had the answer to that, and he took Dana away to give her the good news."

"She went with him?"

"Does a newborn colt go with its mother? That smooth talker just snatched her right from under your nose." Josie looked pleased and angry to have been right.

"Nobody's snatching Dana from anywhere."

"That's not what she said."

Something inside Gabe clamped down hard and fast. "What do you mean?"

"I heard her tell him not to worry, she'd be back in New York soon. She'd turn the whole thing over to her father's lawyers, it would be over in a few days. She said she'd been trying to catch him for five years. She said if she'd known leaving town and getting married would have worked so easily, she'd have done it years ago. Then she kissed him, laughed as if she hadn't a care in the world, and kissed him again. Then she said, 'Now let's run away and hide.'''

"That could mean anything," he repeated.

"Don't be a bigger fool than you already are," Josie snapped. "She's getting ready to leave you, Gabe Purvis. Unless you do something about it, you're going to be raising that kid by yourself."

But he couldn't do anything about it. He'd promised her a divorce when she'd agreed to the marriage. If she wanted one, he would have to give it to her.

He cursed himself for being a fool for waiting so long to ask Dana to stay with him, but it looked as if Fate had been on his side for a change. Apparently she'd realized she didn't love him after all. Seeing her friends from New York made her realize Iron Springs had been a mirage that vanished as soon as an old flame came on the horizon. He couldn't blame Dana for making such a mistake. He'd done it twice. He was just lucky he'd found out before he gave her his heart.

Then why did it feel broken?

Dana picked up the picture of Danny from the bedside table. It had been taken three months earlier when she and Mattie had spent a weekend at her parents's cabin in the Adirondacks. Danny had insisted on helping Mattie gather wood for the fire. He held three small sticks clutched to his chest, a proud grin on his face. Dana looked at the picture for a moment then hugged it to her chest.

She couldn't believe that in a few hours she would be leaving Iron Springs, leaving Danny behind. He had become such an integral part of her life she didn't know how she could go back to living without seeing his face light up when she came into a room, without his throwing his arms around her neck and squeezing as hard as he could, without his saying *I love you, Danie*. She'd miss his soft warmth when she kissed him good night. She'd miss so many little things that had seemed small and inconsequential at the time but seemed monumental now that she faced losing them. Watching him steal sausage from Gabe's plate and stuff it into his mouth before Gabe could steal it back. Finding him in the bathroom with his face covered with shaving cream trying to shave like Gabe. She had known this day would come. She'd tried to prepare for it, but nothing could fortify her against the stark, cold, numbing reality of leaving Danny.

And Gabe.

Dana looked around her at their bedroom. *Gabe's* bedroom. The judge had awarded him custody of Danny the day before. Several friends had come over that evening, and they'd had a celebration. After everyone left, they'd made love. It had been better than ever.

But he didn't ask her to stay.

They'd gotten up early that morning and had breakfast together. He'd talked of Danny's future, all the things he wanted them to do together year by year until the boy got married.

But he didn't ask her to stay.

She and Danny had had lunch with Gabe at the shop as usual. Sam's wife had sent cake and Billy's mother had tied balloons to the bushes by the front door. Several people had dropped in to congratulate Gabe and Dana on winning custody. Gabe hadn't complained when the celebrating went on so long Danny fell asleep in Dana's arms.

But he didn't ask her to say.

She had to face the obvious. He didn't *intend* to ask her to stay. He might love her. He clearly enjoyed making love to her, but he didn't love her enough to be able to conquer his fear of failing again. Maybe it wasn't that simple. Even if he did love her, maybe he didn't think she could be the kind of wife he wanted. After Ellen, maybe he didn't want a wife. Maybe he had all the family he wanted in Danny.

She opened the suitcase on the bed and began to take her clothes from the drawers. Odd how things crept up on a person so slowly you didn't realize anything was happening. She'd entered this house fully expecting to leave. She'd kept most of her clothes in her suitcase, everything else crammed into one drawer and one corner of the closet. Sometime over the past few weeks, all her clothes had gone into the drawers and her suitcase had been put away in the attic. Even more telling, bit by bit, Gabe's clothes had started to reappear in the bedroom.

In the bathroom her stuff sat side by side with Gabe's in the medicine closet, on the various trays and shelves, in the window. She washed their clothes together, dried them together, folded and put them away at the same time without giving it a second thought. Their robes lay on the bed side by side, their shoes intermingled in the closet. From outward appearances, anyone would think their lives were inextricably linked.

Yet they had always been kept separate.

She threw her underwear into the suitcase and walked over to the window. She could see the swings in the backyard where she often sat while Danny played in the shelter of the massive oak that shaded that corner of the yard. She could see the fence that separated Gabe's yard from Mrs. Elderman's. She worked in her garden in the morning and talked to Dana over the fence. Dana had been uncomfortable at first. Then she discovered that Mrs. Elderman's grandmother had been a member of a Shaker community in Ohio. They spent long hours discussing the value of some of the furniture in Mrs. Elderman's house. She didn't want to sell it, but she liked knowing it was valuable.

Mr. and Mrs. Mawbray lived across the street. He worked down the mountain at the ski lodge. People with summer homes kept his store prosperous during the rest of the year. Mrs. Mawbray had a passion for English literature. Dana had minored in English literature. Dana was certain Mrs. Mawbray knew more than half her professors.

She moved down the street in her mind, checking off the families in each house, noting what she'd learned about them, what she would miss when she left. She wiped away a tear. Crying wouldn't change anything. Besides, she had to finish her packing. She intended to be out of the house before noon.

She didn't know what she'd tell Danny, but she couldn't leave without saying goodbye. He had suffered too many unexplained losses already. She intended to lay lots of stress on her promise to come back. She wanted him to think she would be gone only for a short time, but right now she didn't know how she could stand coming face-to-face with everything she'd ever wanted, knowing she couldn't have it.

The other people in town—Mrs. Purvis, Salome, Naomi, all the others who'd gradually become part of her life—would have to do without an explanation. She would let Gabe tell his mother and she could tell everyone else. Just thinking about it caused the tears to start.

She wiped them away and started packing as quickly as she could. She didn't know what she'd do when she came back. Maybe she'd have Gabe bring Danny out to the farmhouse so she wouldn't have to face the people in town. No. He'd have to bring Danny to New York. She couldn't come back to Iron Springs at all.

She was crying so hard by now she couldn't see to pack her clothes. She just grabbed things and stuffed them into the suitcases. It didn't matter if her clothes were ruined. Or if she fled the house and left them behind. She could buy more. Her life was a wreck. She couldn't buy another one of those. She'd been given one chance, and she'd lost it.

"What are you doing?"

The sound of Gabe's voice caused her heart to stop beating. She had meant to leave without seeing him. This was one goodbye she couldn't handle.

Now she didn't have a choice. He was here. He could see what she was doing.

"I'm packing," she answered without turning around. She turned to the closet. She wiped her eyes at the same time she took down several dresses. Without looking up, she carried them to her suitcase and put them in.

"Do you call stuffing designer dresses into a suitcase like they were old rags packing?"

She looked at what she had done. She hadn't even attempted to fold the dresses. She'd simply stuffed them in the suitcase like dirty clothes.

"I'll get them pressed when I get home." Home! Iron Springs was home. New York felt like exile.

"They'll be ruined."

"I'll buy more." It was cruel for him to be worried about her clothes when he didn't care her heart was breaking.

He took the dresses out of the suitcase and hung them

back in the closet. "They won't get wrinkled if you leave them in the closet."

If he thought she was going to come back every weekend like nothing had changed, he was an idiot. If he needed someone to keep pretending to be his wife, he would have to look elsewhere. She'd served her tour of duty. It had cost her more than she could ever have guessed.

She took the dresses and stuffed them back into the suitcase. "There's no reason to leave them here. There's not much chance they'll fit your next girlfriend."

He took the clothes and hung them back in the closet. "They fit the only girlfriend I ever want."

And who the hell was that? "Tell her to get her own clothes." Dana reached for the dresses once more, but Gabe grabbed her wrist. This whole scene was crazy, her taking clothes out of the closet and him putting them back. She felt like she was in a comedy sketch.

"I'm trying to tell you I want you to stay," Gabe said. "Apparently I'm not doing it very well."

"If you want a woman to stay, you say, *Please stay.* You don't keep grabbing her clothes from her hands." She tried to turn away, but he took her by the shoulders, turned her in his direction. When she wouldn't look at him, he put a hand under her chin and tilted her face upward.

"Please stay."

She couldn't believe him. He'd had too many chances to ask her before now. "Why? You don't love me."

"No, I don't love you."

She knew it. He just wanted her to stay so he could keep Danny. Well she wanted him to have Danny, but she couldn't stay, not even if it meant Lucius would get custody. She could shoot Lucius and escape to Paris or the Far East with her father.

"I don't love you," he said again. "I adore you. And even if you don't adore me, don't go with Kyle. He can't love you as much as Danny and I love you."

"I don't know what you're talking about." She knew she was upset, but her brain usually worked better than this.

"I know I can't offer you any of the things Kyle can. I'm not rich, I don't know any billionaires, and I can't give you an apartment in Paris, but I'm offering everything I've got."

She was understanding less and less.

"Your parents sent him, didn't they? They told him about our marriage. They told him you'd be free in a few days. That's why he came. That's why you went off with him."

"Where…how did you know that?" Her mind felt paralyzed.

"Josie told me."

She began to understand. Apparently jealousy had finally shattered the lock on his heart.

"Kyle doesn't love me nearly as much as he loves himself. And money. I've been trying to get him to join Sheila and me in a partnership. He finally agreed if I could talk you into giving us exclusive rights to your furniture. He also agreed to put up the money for expansion. We'll open a showroom in Virginia."

"Then you don't want to marry him?"

Pure jealousy. Now he'd probably start looking for a way to retract every word. "I never wanted to marry Kyle. He's twice as selfish as you and three times as ambitious as I am. Now you'd better go see about Danny's dinner. I've got to finish my packing."

He looked stunned. "Haven't you heard a word I'v[e] been saying. I love you. I want you to stay."

"What I heard, Gabe, was jealousy. You don't want me for yourself, but you'll be damned if anybody is going to steal me from you."

"That's not what I meant."

"How can I believe that? I poured out my heart to you, and you said nothing. Yet the first time you think another man wants me, you fall all over yourself with declarations of love. That's not my idea of love. That's plain old territorial imperative."

"That's not the way it is. I wanted to tell you."

"Tell me what?"

"That I'm crazy about you. That if you leave, I'll have to go after you and bring you back."

She reined in her galloping hope. "You don't have to worry about Danny. He's adjusting very quickly. He'll probably forget me in a few months. Within a year he won't remember me at all."

"I don't want you for Danny," Gabe said. "I want you for myself."

"No, you don't." She prayed he would contradict her. "I've been talking about going back to New York for weeks, hoping every time you'd say something, *anything,* to let me know you wanted me to stay, but you never said a word. Not a single word."

"I was afraid."

"Gabe Purvis, you're not afraid of anybody or anything. Given half a chance, you'd thumb your nose at the world. You probably already have."

"I don't give a damn about the rest of the world, but I'm scared to death of being in love with you."

"Why?"

"I'm not sure. I just am."

A man in love ought to know his mind better than that, or a woman would be a fool to marry him. She reached for her dresses. "When you figure it out, give me a call."

He gripped her hand once more, wouldn't let her remove the dresses from the closet.

"I've never wanted anything in my whole life so much as I want you. I've told myself all the reasons I can't have you, why it won't work, but I can't give up. I'm in love with you. I want to marry you."

She couldn't contain hope any longer. "We're already married."

"I mean *really* married. I want you to stay here, forever."

He had stuck to his story for five minutes. Maybe he did love her. Maybe he did want her to stay, but on what terms. "As you said, we're different. We want different things."

"That's not important anymore."

When a man said his life's work wasn't important, he was either lying or having a mental breakdown. Either case didn't make for good husband material. But she was willing to be convinced. "Why isn't it important?"

"Because I love you!" he nearly shouted. "I'll go anywhere you want me to as long as you will let me love you for the rest of my life."

She didn't believe that for a minute. Gabe Purvis was the last man in the world to knuckle under to anybody, but she liked hearing it. Maybe he had finally learned to let emotion get the better of his common sense. A good sign.

"What about my career?"

"We'll work out something."

"I'll have to travel to New York from time to time."

"I'll need to go to show my furniture, to talk to buyers about orders."

Suddenly she didn't feel the slightest bit interested in being obstreperous. Everything she wanted was almost in reach. She could feel herself letting go inside. She had to make sure it was genuine before her heart burst with happiness.

"Do you love me, Gabe? I mean really, *honestly* love me. The woman inside, not all the things on the outside."

"It was all those *things* that scared me to death." He took the hands she'd clenched together and held them tightly in his own. "How could I help but love the woman inside. She's honest, courageous and trustworthy. She's also been underappreciated most of her life. I intend to spend the rest of my life telling you how wonderful I think you are. I know you think jealousy caused me to say this, but it was seeing you at the fair. You were surrounded by people I didn't know. I felt like you were moving farther and farther away from me every minute. That's when I knew no matter what it cost, I couldn't let you leave."

"Why didn't you tell me any of this before now?"

"I was afraid to break out of the rut I've been in for fifteen years. I was afraid to trust my heart to anyone's keeping. But I wanted to. When I saw you pulling away from me, I knew I had to do something, *anything*, to keep you from leaving me."

Dana had trouble talking around the lump in her throat. "All you had to do was ask. Was that so hard?"

"It was the hardest thing I've ever done. Now stop giving me the third degree and say you'll marry me."

"We're already married," Dana managed to say before her throat closed.

"I know, but we'll have to think of something to make it feel real this time."

"My love is very real. There's nothing childish about it this time. I love you physically, how you make me feel when we make love. But I also love what you stand for as a man, your commitment to Sam and Billy and the community. I love what we've made together, you, me and Danny. I don't know why it took me so long to figure that out, but it's what I've been looking for all my life. It's why I kept coming back to my grandmother's all those summers when my mother wanted to send me to camp. It's why Mattie and I were such good friends. I suppose it's why I never really forgot you."

They didn't talk for several minutes. "What are you doing to do about those dresses?" Gabe asked when he finally stopped kissing her.

"I don't know." They looked hopelessly crumpled. "Maybe I'll keep them to remind me how close we came to losing everything."

Gabe held her a little closer. "You never had a chance of getting away. I'd have hitchhiked all the way to New York if necessary."

Dana hooted. "You'd never have survived the New Jersey Turnpike."

"With a couple of rifles over my shoulder and several hunting knives hanging from my belt, I don't think anybody would have bothered me. When a mountain man goes hunting his woman, he's downright serious."

Dana smiled happily. She was a very fortunate woman. She had it all, and she meant to hold it very close. It had been a long time in coming. She intended to treasure every moment.

For at least the next fifty years.

*   *   *   *   *

PAMELA TOTH
DIANA WHITNEY
ALLISON LEIGH
LAURIE PAIGE

bring you four heartwarming stories in the brand-new series

So Many Babies

At the Buttonwood Baby Clinic,
babies and romance abound!

On sale January 2000: **THE BABY LEGACY**
by Pamela Toth

On sale February 2000: **WHO'S THAT BABY?**
by Diana Whitney

On sale March 2000: **MILLIONAIRE'S INSTANT BABY**
by Allison Leigh

On sale April 2000: **MAKE WAY FOR BABIES!**
by Laurie Paige

Only from Silhouette **SPECIAL EDITION**
Available at your favorite retail outlet.

Silhouette®
Where love comes alive™

If you enjoyed what you just read,
then we've got an offer you can't resist!

Take 2 bestselling love stories FREE!

Plus get a FREE surprise gift!

Clip this page and mail it to Silhouette Reader Service™

IN U.S.A.	IN CANADA
3010 Walden Ave.	P.O. Box 609
P.O. Box 1867	Fort Erie, Ontario
Buffalo, N.Y. 14240-1867	L2A 5X3

YES! Please send me 2 free Silhouette Special Edition® novels and my free surprise gift. Then send me 6 brand-new novels every month, which I will receive months before they're available in stores. In the U.S.A., bill me at the bargain price of $3.57 plus 25¢ delivery per book and applicable sales tax, if any*. In Canada, bill me at the bargain price of $3.96 plus 25¢ delivery per book and applicable taxes**. That's the complete price and a savings of over 10% off the cover prices—what a great deal! I understand that accepting the 2 free books and gift places me under no obligation ever to buy any books. I can always return a shipment and cancel at any time. Even if I never buy another book from Silhouette, the 2 free books and gift are mine to keep forever. So why not take us up on our invitation. You'll be glad you did!

235 SEN CNFD
335 SEN CNFE

Name	(PLEASE PRINT)	
Address	Apt.#	
City	State/Prov.	Zip/Postal Code

* Terms and prices subject to change without notice. Sales tax applicable in N.Y.
** Canadian residents will be charged applicable provincial taxes and GST.
All orders subject to approval. Offer limited to one per household.
® are registered trademarks of Harlequin Enterprises Limited.

SPED99   ©1998 Harlequin Enterprises Limited

Silhouette Special Edition brings you

by SHERRYL WOODS

AND BABY MAKES THREE

The Delacourts of Texas

*Come join the Delacourt family as they all find love—
and parenthood—in the most unexpected ways!*

On sale December 1999:
THE COWBOY AND THE NEW YEAR'S BABY (SE#1291)
During one of the worst blizzards in Texas history, a
stranded Trish Delacourt was about to give birth! Luckily,
sexy Hardy Jones rushed to the rescue. Could the no-strings
bachelor and the new mom turn a precious New Year's
miracle into a labor of *love?*

On sale March 2000:
DYLAN AND THE BABY DOCTOR (SE#1309)
Private detective Dylan Delacourt had closed off part of
his heart and wasn't prepared for what Kelsey James stirred
up when she called on him to locate her missing son.

And don't miss Jeb Delacourt's story coming
to Special Edition in July 2000.

Silhouette®
Where love comes alive™

Available at your favorite retail outlet.

Start celebrating Silhouette's 20th anniversary
with these 4 special titles by
New York Times bestselling authors

*Fire and Rain**
by Elizabeth Lowell

King of the Castle
by Heather Graham Pozzessere

*State Secrets**
by Linda Lael Miller

*Paint Me Rainbows**
by Fern Michaels

On sale in December 1999

Available at your favorite retail outlet
**Also available on audio from Brilliance.*

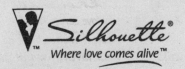

**Special Edition is celebrating
Silhouette's 20th anniversary!**

Special Edition brings you:

• brand-new **LONG, TALL TEXANS**
Matt Caldwell: Texas Tycoon by **Diana Palmer**
(January 2000)

• a bestselling miniseries
PRESCRIPTION: MARRIAGE
(December 1999-February 2000)
Marriage may be just what the doctor ordered!

• a brand-new miniseries **SO MANY BABIES**
(January-April 2000)
At the Buttonwood Baby Clinic,
lots of babies—and love—abound

• the exciting conclusion of **ROYALLY WED!**
(February 2000)

• the new **AND BABY MAKES THREE:
THE DELACOURTS OF TEXAS**
by **Sherryl Woods**
(December 1999, March & July 2000)

And on sale in June 2000, don't miss
Nora Roberts' brand-new story
Irish Rebel
in **Special Edition**.

Available at your favorite retail outlet.

Where love comes alive™

Visit us at www.romance.net   PS20SSE_R